Pleasure
PLANET

Claire Thompson
Beverly Havlir

Ellora's Cave
Romantica Publishing

D1214324

An Ellora's Cave Romantica Publication

www.ellorascave.com

Pleasure Planet

ISBN # 1419952870
ALL RIGHTS RESERVED.
Eros Copyright © 2005 Claire Thompson
Tristan's Woman Copyright © 2005 Beverly Havlir

Edited by: Mary Moran and Heather Osborn
Cover art by: Syneca

Electronic book Publication: May, 2005
Trade paperback Publication: November, 2005

With the exception of quotes used in reviews, this book may not be reproduced or used in whole or in part by any means existing without written permission from the publisher, Ellora's Cave Publishing, Inc.® 1056 Home Avenue, Akron OH 44310-3502.

This book is a work of fiction and any resemblance to persons, living or dead, or places, events or locales is purely coincidental. The characters are productions of the authors' imagination and used fictitiously.

DETROIT PUBLIC LIBRARY

3 5674 04669258 9

What the critics are saying...

Pleasure Factor 5 cupids "...The sex scene are spicy and romantic... Eros is a very enjoyable novella that left me satisfied with no loose ends. *Ms. Thompson's* stories are always a pleasure to read for me and she did not disappoint in this one!" ~ *Luisa for Cupid's Library Reviews*

4 *Angels* "...This interesting tale deals with what happens when we get what we wish for...The emotional connection between Asia and Ronan will draw you in as they each find themselves in a relationship they do not want to lose *Tewanda for Fallen Angel Reviews*

"...A sp   rt to a hot book, *Eros* is sure to please... *Claire Thomp*   s written an impressive tale chock full of realistic cl   rs and emotions, steamy, raw sex, and adventure." ~   *a Camp for Romance Reviews Today*

4/5 *Stars*   ..Set in a future with technology far superior to our own, the science fiction element adds an imaginative and sensual flare to the plot. The sex scenes include some spicy...BDSM elements...This extremely seductive novella kept my interest all the way through the story and left me feeling satisfied and invigorated. ~ *Francesca Hayne for JERR*

DEC _ 2007

HUBBARD BRANCH LIBRARY
12929 W. McNICHOLS
DETROIT, MI 48235
578-7585

"…an enjoyable, sensual piece of work. This futurist love story, set in the twenty-fourth century, explores the world of submission. This is an intense story that is a true erotic piece of literature. *Pleasure Planet: Eros* is a fascinating story that will leave readers eager and hungry for more." ~ *Chantay for Euro-Reviews*

5 Stars "…Eros is filled with twists and plot turns while telling a story so hot it nearly scorches the pages. Turn up your AC, grab a cold drink, and sit back to enjoy the ride." ~ *Cindy Warner for Coffee Time Romance*

Warning:

The following material contains graphic sexual content meant for mature readers. *Pleasure Planet* has been rated *E-rotic* by a minimum of three independent reviewers.

Ellora's Cave Publishing offers three levels of Romantica™ reading entertainment: S (S-ensuous), E (E-rotic), and X (X-treme).

S-*ensuous* love scenes are explicit and leave nothing to the imagination.

E-*rotic* love scenes are explicit, leave nothing to the imagination, and are high in volume per the overall word count. In addition, some E-rated titles might contain fantasy material that some readers find objectionable, such as bondage, submission, same sex encounters, forced seductions, etc. E-rated titles are the most graphic titles we carry; it is common, for instance, for an author to use words such as "fucking", "cock", "pussy", etc., within their work of literature.

X-*treme* titles differ from E-rated titles only in plot premise and storyline execution. Unlike E-rated titles, stories designated with the letter X tend to contain controversial subject matter not for the faint of heart.

Contents

Eros

Claire Thompson

Chapter One

Aria looked around with curiosity. She'd been on the waiting list for this trip for three New Earth months and she supposed that must mean this was the place to be. She flicked her scarf over her shoulder, consciously tossing her head to make her silver hair shimmer and glow in the moonlight or whatever light it was they were using to create this ambiance.

She liked her new curls—they were real silver, not that cheap imitation coloring most New Earthians had to use. Aria had connections. She was not only heiress to the Moon Flights fortune but had made her own wealth with her innovative designs in space travel suitcases for the traveler on the go. The patented shrinkware reduced bulky cases to the size of a slim makeup bag with the touch of the shrinkwand. It was programmed via retinal scan for security and made it possible to pack a decent number of outfits—for Aria this meant at least two changes of clothing a day—for whatever trip you made, no matter how backward the spaceship or planetary accommodations of your destination.

Aria had expected to disembark at a typical spaceport, bustling with porters and various species collecting their baggage and hurrying for taxis. But when her autoship had docked and the door slid soundlessly open, she found herself on some kind of beach! She stepped hesitantly down the ship's walkway, wondering briefly if her coordinates had been faulty. She checked her pocket locator but it indicated that she was in fact on the continent of Eros, on this planet of pleasure. The atmosphere was clearly suitable for humans and she took a deep breath of slightly salty air.

As she stepped onto the ground, the sand was smooth and white, cool to the touch. The sound of the waves crashing in the distance reminded her of Galana, her home city on New Earth. In fact, this could *be* Galana. It even smelled right.

Though she had traveled extensively throughout this and neighboring galaxies, Aria was had never entirely gotten used to the alien smell of other planets. Of course, it was rude to comment and eventually one got used to it.

This homey scent was a pleasant surprise indeed! As she looked toward the little village in the distance, she was disconcerted to see the old temple, its gold-leafed dome gleaming in the moonlight. Again, she glanced at her pocket locator. Had her ship been mis-programmed? Was she in fact back on her home planet?

Then it dawned on her! This was Eros, famous even on this planet of dreams as a premiere continent for personalized pleasure. When she'd completed the questionnaire and allowed the brain scan, of course they'd been able to design her perfect fantasy, right down to the scent of her planet and her favorite place in the entire galaxy, her hometown.

Unlike most of the hedonistic spas where the men—human men in her case, though of course it varied by species and preference—were lined up like licorice whips in a candy store, here on Eros you were assigned an "ideal mate"—someone pulled right out of your dreams.

She'd been subjected to a complete physical examination, to assure that she could "withstand" the excitement promised in the sales literature. Of course, she received the birth control inoculations, though she wondered a bit at this, since as far as she knew, different species couldn't procreate. She'd been forced to attend the requisite seminars, detailing the risks of such an involvement and she'd had to sign the palmwriter waivers absolving the planet of any responsibility for a broken heart.

This had excited Aria as was probably the intention. It must be a really authentic experience if they felt the need for so many warnings and disclaimers. However, unlike the real thing, once the week was up, it was so long and farewell. This suited Aria perfectly since she had no intention of falling in love for many years to come. At thirty-two, she was only a little over one-fifth through her expected life span so what was the rush?

Aria was distracted from her thoughts by the lovely sound of a flute wafting along the warm night breeze. She followed the sound, knowing somehow that it was meant for her. The sand was cool and inviting and she slipped off her sandals, carrying them in one hand as she drew closer to the sweet notes of what sounded like a Galanian love chant.

A small house came into view, cut from pale blue stone. A curl of smoke rose from a little chimney that poked through the red tiled roof. How charming! A fireplace. That delightful old-fashioned way of providing heat. Aria had always been enchanted by fireplaces and had them built into several of her homes. She had even learned how to make a fire, using carbon composite rods that looked like the logs in the ancient texts. Logs, she knew, came from those plants called "trees" that had once existed in abundance on Old Earth. Most of her friends had thought her quaint but then she was never one to march to others' drums.

Aria approached the little house and stood at the door, wondering if she should knock or just walk right in. Finally, she lifted the little gold knocker and let it fall against the door. The music stopped and after a moment, the door opened.

Aria drew in her breath, her eyes widening in surprise. It was Doran! Her very first lover, from Eshelon. New Earth's sister planet. They had met at university, and she had fallen head over heels for the boy with the intensity that only first love can bring.

When he'd graduated and signed on to a science vessel that was making a five-year journey to another galaxy, Aria had been devastated. He'd chosen his career over her. In what would become a pattern for her, Aria turned her back on him, hardening her heart and closing her mind. She deleted the letters he sent her, without even opening the files.

She didn't need a man, she told herself and anyone who would listen. She was Aria Loran, an independent woman of the twenty-fourth century! But now, faced with Doran in the flesh, she felt faint and disoriented. It was Doran, wasn't it? Yet he still looked as young as the day they'd parted. The golden hair, luminous and shining in the soft light. The large eyes, thin patrician nose and lips. This man wasn't dressed as Doran used to, in the silver unisuits that were so popular at school, sported by men and women alike. No, this fellow was dressed in some soft shimmery fabric that seemed to change color as he moved. The shirt was tailored like the ancient pirates of old, with the full sleeves and open collar, revealing a manly, broad chest tanned to a golden bronze. Instead of Doran's large blue eyes, she saw that this man's irises were golden—the telltale mark of the Erosian species.

"Welcome, Aria. I am your guide for this week of pleasure. You may call me Ronan or Doran, if you wish." After all this time, even though she rarely thought of Doran at all, the Erosians had created what they must have believed was her "perfect man".

She smiled, taking the man's offered hand and said, "I'd rather call you Ronan, thank you."

Ronan led her through the rustic living room, which held several overstuffed sofas and brightly woven throw rugs covering a smooth stone floor. She saw that one wall was entirely transparent, revealing a tumultuous sea under the dark Erosian sky.

Leading her to a smaller enclosed alcove, Ronan gestured to a round dining table, which was set for two. As Aria sat, he poured a dark red drink into the two waiting goblets. "A local wine I think you'll find pleasant," he remarked, raising his glass in a toast to the young woman.

Smiling, she took a sip of the offered drink. It was delicious, but made her realize she was ravenously hungry. As if reading her mind Ronan brought a tray from the counter and set several of Aria's favorite foods in front of her, including the New Earth peaches and raspberries she loved and a variety of Andromeda cheeses and caviars. The freshly baked bread smelled wonderful. She broke off a small piece, spreading some of the soft pungent cheese across a still-warm slice.

"This is delicious," she enthused, smiling at Ronan. So far, so good. Fabulous food in a beautiful but casual setting with a gorgeous man, though she wished he wasn't quite so precise a copy of Doran.

She glanced out at the ocean view as she took another drink of her wine. When she turned back to her host, it appeared that her wish had been his command. She saw that his features had changed. Not so much so that he wasn't recognizable, but the nose was longer and wider, the lips fuller, the hair darkened to a light brown, now only highlighted with gold. This slightly altered version simply reminded her of the old Doran but was no longer his carbon copy. She found this new model was actually more pleasing to the mature eye. Less obviously "perfect" and more manly as a result.

"Wow!" she exclaimed, impressed. "You guys really do aim to please!"

Ronan bowed slightly. "My apologies on the first image, my lady. Your brain scan indicated that it would be ideal, but sometimes there are inaccuracies."

"Well, you're perfect now, Ronan. Don't change a thing."

"I shan't, at least not at your direction." As Aria cocked an eyebrow quizzically, he added, "Your week has now officially begun. You are no longer a paying visitor at a luxury spa. You are my sexual prisoner. My love slave, and I shall do exactly as I please, with or without your consent."

"What!" Aria's eyes flashed. What was this impertinent servant talking about! She was Aria Loran, one of the richest women in the galaxy! No one talked to her in that tone! No one gave her orders! Sex slave? Was the man mad! She'd call the manager! She'd demand a refund!

"Methinks the lady doth protest too much," Ronan said quietly, a smile on his lips. She recognized the ancient Bard's quote, and realized with annoyance the man was reading her mind. She had known that Erosians were telepathic but hadn't given the matter much thought until now. Was nothing to be private here?

"Nothing," Ronan replied, smiling. "In fact, you belong to me, Aria. Completely. We are alone here. There is no manager or other 'superior' to whom you can appeal. My word is law — at least for this week — we are committed to one another. Your communication devices are inoperative here. You are completely at my mercy. I am physically much stronger than you are and this is my domain. You may as well accept it."

Aria stared at him, her eyes wide. A terrible mistake? A kidnapping for ransom? Was he going to kill her? Where was her dream lover, the one she'd paid so handsomely for? Ronan stood and walked over to Aria. He knelt next to her and wrapped his strong arms around her. Pulling her face gently down, he kissed her lips — a long, lingering kiss that left her breathless.

She felt heat between her legs. This man's love slave! His prisoner. She blushed now, realizing what had happened. The brain scan had revealed what Aria had never told a soul. What she had barely admitted to herself. Her most secret fantasy of all — to be taken prisoner by a gorgeous man and held under his control as he had his way with her!

She had never admitted to this fantasy because it didn't match her own self-image of a strong and independent woman. Men and women were complete equals in society now, though it had taken thousands of years to finally achieve. Not only was she equal to a man in every way, she was vastly superior to most in terms of wealth and power. Every man she'd dated since Doran had respected her power and authority.

On the surface, this suited Aria but in a secret part of her soul, she longed to be controlled. To be "taken" by a strong man who knew what he wanted and wasn't afraid to demand it.

Her conscious sexual fantasies were more traditional for a woman of her stature and times. Here on this "pleasure planet" as it was nicknamed, she had thought she would be provided with lots of attention and adoration, and perhaps multiple partners, both men and women, over the course of the week. She had imagined one long orgy of self-indulgence and pleasure.

But now, faced with this swashbuckling fellow in his silk pirate shirt and the rakish gleam in his eye, she realized she was to have a very different week indeed! They'd delved further into her psyche than perhaps she cared for, and now it seemed she would have no say in the matter!

Ronan stood and held out his hand, a clear command for her to stand and accept it. She did so, annoyed that her fingers trembled slightly. This was just a fantasy, a game! He was going to be her captor, her love jailer, and subject her to all sorts of glorious sexual games. Well, that sounded wonderful! It was just a game, after all. As Aria followed him into the living room, she smiled at the sight of the fire that was crackling in the grate.

She was distracted from taking in the comfortable furniture and the wide bay windows that let in the starlight into the room, by his command. "Strip."

Aria stared up at the man, certain she had misheard. There was time, surely, and in the bedroom! He interrupted her thoughts, "I said, strip!" His tone was sharp, brooking no disobedience. Aria started to protest and Ronan, taking the edge of her scarf, pulled it from her. Then his large hands found the hidden zippers on the sides of her gown and pulled them down so that the dress flapped open, revealing the naked body beneath it.

Horrified, Aria grabbed at her dress, trying to cover herself. This was too much! Calmly Ronan said, "Stop with the performance, Aria. It's only you and me now. There's no one to put on the 'powerful woman affronted' show for. I gave you a simple command. You failed to obey it. Next time, you'll get a spanking for that. This time, I'm letting it slide."

Forcing her arms high over her head with one hand, Ronan lifted the flimsy garment up and off the dumbfounded woman. Aria stood naked, her long silver hair curling down her back, gleaming softly in the firelight. Her round, firm breasts were tipped with dark pink nipples that were poking to attention as Ronan gazed at his captive.

Dropping her wrists, Ronan stepped back. "You're beautiful," he murmured, and it sounded heartfelt. "Don't fight me, darling girl. Surrender. This is your dream. Revel in it." Aria covered her body protectively, in the classic pose with one hand over her silver pubic mound and the other trying ineffectually to hide her breasts.

She was trembling, trying to catch her breath. Ronan pulled her to him, locking her in his embrace. He whispered in her ear, "Aria. Aria. Calm yourself. You're shivering. All you need to do is relax and to obey me. I won't demand anything of you that you don't already want—don't already crave. Sometimes our fantasies aren't clear, even to ourselves. I'll help you to unlock them. You can trust me, my love. I exist solely for you."

Slowly her heart stopped its insistent hammering against her ribs. Her breathing eased as the strong man held her in his arms. She leaned her head against his shoulder and realized he smelled nice. Not like Doran, but with his own scent, something warm and spicy, almost like cloves, but lighter.

That's right, she reminded herself, *he exists solely for me!* This was her week! She'd paid an extraordinary sum for the peculiar adventure now facing her. The reputation of the place was stellar. The Erosians must know what they were doing. This man wasn't her kidnapper, he was really *her* sex slave as it was her money that had purchased this lark. He could pretend to be her lord and master all he liked. She knew the real situation.

And if damsel in distress was the fantasy they were going to play, well, why not? It would be fun! Ronan's hands, which had been gripping her bare shoulders, dropped now to her ass. He cupped the round globes and squeezed.

"Think what you like, Aria. It may only be a week but it's going to be much more than a game, I assure you. Yes, you bought the time and the experience, but you cannot just turn it off at your whim. Now you have to play by the rules—my rules.

"I'm going to give you pleasure you've never experienced before. I promise you that. I know you're used to getting exactly what you want, exactly when you want it. That may not be the case this week. I'm going to test you. And as with any test worth its merit, there will be rewards as well as punishments. Real punishments, not playacting. I'm going to take you beyond the limits you've set with your conscious mind. Do you understand what I'm saying?"

Aria surveyed the handsome man before her. This lovely specimen of male human perfection was giving her the "script" for their luscious little game. He was laying out the rules by which he would pretend to be her lord and master. Slowly she nodded, smiling slightly. She did feel at somewhat of a disadvantage since she was now naked and he was fully clothed. Still, she knew men, at least human men, found her quite attractive and she was proud of her firm, strong body.

She had paid a pretty penny for this week! She might as well relax and enjoy it. Obviously, his posturing was all an act, how could it be otherwise? Though, he had sounded so serious as he gave his little speech. "Punishments", indeed! The fellow wouldn't dare to really punish her! She'd have the whole planet shut down! Let him play his games. She would stand up to him, play by play.

If Ronan was reading her mind as these thoughts scrolled through it, he gave no indication. Gently he forced her to sit down on the couch. Kneeling between her knees, he spread her thighs with his large hands.

"A few rules, my love. You will address me with respect. You will call me Ronan or Sir. You will thank me for each thing I do to you, whether you like it or not. You will obey each directive immediately or you will be punished. Do I make myself clear?"

As he spoke, Ronan was staring at Aria's silvery pubic curls, which had been perfectly colored to match the hair on her head. She found herself blushing furiously as he impassively eyed her bared pussy, the delicate folds peeking from under the curls. She tried to close her legs but his strong hands were upon her. He knelt down so that she could feel his breath against her skin. She felt her blood stirring like metal to a magnet. She knew she was wet and this embarrassed her all the more.

She wouldn't put up with this! Fantasy was one thing, but this was entirely too real for her taste or comfort. "I demand a refund!" she snapped. This new feeling of a loss of control made her words more sharp than she intended. And even as she protested, she couldn't ignore the sexual desire blooming through her at this man's dominant display. Still trying to hold onto her dignity she added, though with less conviction, "This is outrageous. You're holding me against my will."

"Oh, Aria. Aria. Hush now with this foolishness. I told you before," his voice was slow and patient, as if he were trying to explain something to a small and somewhat stupid child. "There is no one to whom you can appeal. I own you now. You can stamp those pretty little feet all you like. You can demand whatever you want, but it's not going to get you anywhere. Except over my knee for a good spanking. Now, I'm being more than patient because we've only just begun and I can see you are little slow."

"How dare you!" This was too much! *Slow?!* She had been in the top one percent at university and she ran one of the largest corporations in the galaxy! *Slow?!* The audacity! When she got this straightened out, this Erosian would never work in this spa or anywhere else again! She would see to it. She stared at him now, aware that he was reading her mind as plainly as if she were speaking aloud. This infuriated her all the more, and impulsively, she slapped his face.

Ronan's head twisted, his eyes registering his surprise and pain. Apparently, her impulse hadn't articulated itself in her mind and Ronan was caught by surprise. Aria held her breath, the first trickle of real fear dripping into her veins.

Touching his cheek, Ronan stared at Aria for a moment. His golden eyes looked darker, almost brown. He seemed to be gathering his thoughts. Finally, he said, "You still do not understand, Aria. I can see words are wasted on you, though you humans must rely on them so heavily. Very well. I'll stop explaining. What is that human expression, 'actions speak louder than words'?"

He sat next to Aria on the couch. She wrapped her arms protectively around herself turning her head away. As if lifting a pillow or a small child, Ronan easily pulled her across his firm thighs so that her bottom was lifted for the hand that now fell heavily across it. Aria screamed. This was no pretend spanking by a pretend pirate. It was a very real, and very hard swatting! Aria tried to slip from his lap but he held her down, gripping her head between his knees, and keeping one hand firmly against the small of her back. In addition to the sting of his hard palm against her, Aria felt humiliated to be held down in this ignoble position. Again and again he smacked her ass until Aria finally went limp from the struggle and tears were streaming down her soft cheeks.

Only then, did Ronan pull her up onto his lap and cradle her, smoothing her tears with his fingers and kissing them away. In a soft voice he said, "You see, my love. I will punish you if you disobey me. The sooner you learn that, the better things will go for you. Now, what do you say?"

Aria sniffed loudly. She didn't answer.

"I said," Ronan took her chin in his fingers and forced her to look at him, "what do you say? You are to thank me for each action, whether it be punishment or pleasure. And remember to properly address me."

Aria started to struggle against him, her eyes flashing, but her very sore and tender bottom made her think the better of it and meekly she said, "Thank you, Ronan."

Chapter Two

Ronan stood with Aria still in his arms, and carried her into the bedroom. Most of the room was filled by the large bed, raised high on a dais. It was draped with pretty, bright silks over a canopy of black iron-like material. The drapes parted of their own accord as they approached and Ronan laid his slave girl on the bed. The mattress immediately conformed to her body's contour. It was quite the most comfortable thing Aria had ever lain upon. If she hadn't been so disconcerted and overwhelmed by what was happening to her, she would have curled up and gone right to sleep.

Sighing, Aria closed her eyes, fatigue suddenly weighing her down. The space flight had taken its toll. It had been a long day and the moons over Eros were already setting. Her bottom still stung from the spanking and yet, at the same time, she couldn't deny the heat of arousal in her sex. That spanking had loosened something in her. Something wound tight and held very close inside of her.

Once she had gotten over Doran, she had fancied herself very much in control. While she had had many lovers over the years and considered herself experienced, she also felt she was impervious. No man could actually reach her heart, and this had suited her perfectly.

This week was to have been just another enjoyable diversion in a series of sexual releases that a woman of her position and responsibility needed in order to relax and work at the top of her form. Now she gently rubbed her sore bottom. That spanking hadn't been a playful swatting. She would probably bruise! How dare he? She knew she should feel more outrage than she in fact did.

She also knew this man, this alien, whatever he was, could see into her mind. Past her mind it seemed, and into her secret fantasies. He had treated her in a way no man had ever dared. And she couldn't deny it—it *was* thrilling, in a certain way, to know that at last there was someone who dared to stand up to Aria Loran, founder and Chief Executive Officer of Travel Kits Universal. Certainly, no one would have dared in any other circumstance. And yet, she was conflicted. It felt too real. It *was* real, she reminded herself, gingerly touching her tender bottom.

Ronan left Aria alone for a moment, returning with a glass of something to drink. He handed it to her silently and Aria sniffed at it. The scent was something fruity, perhaps fermented, like a wine or mead. It was a dark magenta color, pretty against the pale gold of the cup. "What is it?" she asked.

"It's another Erosian wine. Made from a grape that grows in our mountainous regions to the north. Hopefully it is pleasing to your palette." She sipped the drink. It was delicious! Greedily she drank the entire cup. Her head felt heavy and her body was suddenly beyond fatigued. Ronan pressed her gently back against soft pillows as he took the empty cup from her limp hand.

As her eyelids slid down, her last conscious vision was of the brightly colored silk canopy fluttering gently in the soft ocean breeze coming through an open window.

* * * * *

Aria came awake abruptly. The room was dark, though a hint of stars splashed some incandescent silvery light through the window. For a moment, Aria had no idea where she was. Her body felt delicious, perfectly relaxed. As her mind cleared, she recalled where she was, smack in the middle of this adventure, too sleepy to feel the slightest apprehension.

The mattress gently cradled her body. Though she lay naked with no cover, the room's temperature was perfectly suited to her—warm but fresh with the soft breeze scented by the Erosian Sea.

She felt hands, strong but gentle against her, smoothing the muscles in her thighs and calves. Ronan was stretched out alongside her, though she couldn't make out his features in the semi-dark. She felt his fingers, which gently prodded her to turn over onto her belly. She complied, feeling too peaceful and pleasant to resist. His strong fingers kneaded the muscles of her back and buttocks, eliciting a sigh of sleepy pleasure from the young woman.

She felt as if she were melting back into the bed, a pool of liquid peace. When he gently shifted her to her back, Aria only moaned softly, half asleep. She came awake though as the man pushed her legs apart. His fingers brushed lightly against her spread sex. Instinctively Aria tried to close her legs, but found to her surprise she could not! He wasn't holding her down or even touching her legs at all but she couldn't move them.

"It's a force field," he whispered as he leaned over her, nuzzling her neck with his nose and lightly running his lips down the curve of her collarbone. "Completely harmless. It just renders you, ah, more compliant to my wishes." His kisses were like little whispered love songs, singing along her throat, her collarbone, her breasts. His lips closed lightly over a nipple. She felt his tongue, hot and sweet, against the tender tip.

Aria was able to lift her head as Ronan moved to a position between her still-spread legs. She saw in the pearly light that he was dressed in some kind of sleep garb. It looked to be of light cotton or linen, the shirt cut with a deep V that showed a broad bare chest. She licked her lips at the beautiful sight of him, realizing that she would have liked to tell *him* to strip. He presented as a gorgeous human specimen, whatever his real species might be.

Aria closed her eyes, succumbing at last, for what choice did she have? His tongue was like velvet, sliding softly against her sex, teasing out the moisture, making it flow. Yes, this was what she had paid for—perfect attentions, lovingly given. The fact that she couldn't close her legs, even if she had wanted to, made it more exciting.

She was this man's captive, on a strange planet, completely removed from her entourage of servants, employees and friends. No one could rescue her, if that was what she needed. No, she didn't need rescuing. She needed his lovely tongue, licking hot and hard against her. Though she couldn't close her legs, she found she could arch her hips, and she did so, angling herself to best receive his oral offering.

"Yes," she hissed, low and insistent, as he continued to take her closer to the edge of release. "Yes, do it!" He did, skillfully bringing her to climax and then, after only a moment's respite, doing it again.

Just when she felt she couldn't take another kiss, another smooth heated stroke, the force field was released and she was able to move again. Curling on her side, Aria breathed deeply, feeling the deep languor of sexual satiation settle over her like a net.

Ronan slid up next to her, unfolding his body next to hers. He was still in his sleep garb. Aria found herself wondering sleepily if the Erosian was fully functional as a human male.

Ronan laughed quietly and said into her ear, "Fully, my dear. As you shall soon experience. But not now. You are only dreaming now, my love. Go to sleep, go to sleep." His voice was soothing as he hummed a quiet little tune, something almost familiar, something from long ago that sent Aria into a deep and dreamless sleep. It was, after all, only the first night.

Chapter Three

Breakfast was sumptuous. In addition to Aria's favorite summer fruits, there were fresh muffins, rolls and croissants, and something not unlike the eggs of New Earth, made into a delicious omelet with some kind of mushrooms. The coffee was strong and hot, with fresh cream.

Aria had awoken to the pale orange sunlight of this planet, feeling unusually refreshed. Ronan was nowhere in sight, but she found the bathroom on her own and stepped into the shower. She was perplexed at first, as there were no knobs or familiar control panel, but after a moment, water sprayed hot and fast from the ceiling and walls of the shower stall. She realized the soap and shampoo were already in the water mixture and so she lathered up. At the precise moment she was ready to rinse, the water became clear. She made a mental note to explore the technology for her company.

For now, though, she contented herself with her toilette and then went to find the man she had "purchased" for the week.

"Good morning, sleepyhead." Ronan was sitting at the table, sipping a cup of something fragrant and hot. He was dressed now in white linen pants, rumpled and loose against his strong body. He wore no shirt. Aria saw that he was darkly tanned and his muscles rippled as he lifted his cup.

She realized she was staring and looked toward the food. Seeing the delicious spread, she sat, quickly loading her plate with fruit and bread, accepting Ronan's offer to fill her cup. "Well, good morning to you, Ronan. Or should I say, 'Sir'?" The man's admonitions of the night before—how she must address him with respect and thank him for every act—seemed silly now in the light of day.

Ronan smiled blandly and said, "As you wish, Aria. Nothing has changed since last night. I've been planning our agenda for today."

"Oh?" Aria grinned at him. He could pretend he was her master all he liked, but surely, they both knew who was paying whom.

"Yes. Today we are going to explore your difficulty with letting go. Your intense need to control all situations at all costs."

"I'm sure I don't know what you're talking about," Aria said coldly. "Unless you're referring to the fact that I control a virtual empire of businesses that span over one hundred planets throughout the galaxy. Or the fact that I haven't felt the need to mate or sign a marriage contract with a man." She looked at him defiantly, waiting for his cowed response.

"No, actually. I wasn't referring to that. At least not directly. I was referring to the way you always hold your heart in check. To the way you never completely give of yourself, no matter how intimate a situation might appear to be. And beneath that to your, as yet mostly unexplored submissive nature and desires. That, I think, is the key to setting you free."

Aria felt herself flush and she turned away. "I wasn't aware I needed 'setting free'. You overstep your place, *Sir*."

Ronan smiled gently at Aria, putting his large hand over her much smaller one. His voice was soft, even compelling, as he said, "Aria, my dear. Please. You needn't fight me at every turn. I'm not some competitor for your business or even a lover seeking your permanent attentions. This is your week. If you choose, we can just make it about easy sex and simple satisfaction.

"But you fascinate me. I don't mind telling you, I petitioned for your assignment. Your profile is so complex. Most of the humans I see are after a simple 'good time'. Forgive my bluntness, but they just want an attractive partner to fuck their brains out for a week and then send them on their way. Not that there's anything wrong with that. I appreciate the human need for release and simple pleasures. I even admire it.

"But there was something different about you. Perhaps it's because you're such a high-profile success story — beautiful and independently wealthy — with a high intelligence and a very curious nature. And an underlying, and as yet unexplored, submissive streak that draws me to you, makes me want to test you. To help you release that very sexy aspect of your personality that no other being has tapped into."

Aria was staring at him, her breakfast forgotten. "That was quite a speech," she remarked. She had been pleased with his rather glowing description of her, but she was used to the accolades that went along with success. More, she was intrigued with his references to her sexual submissiveness. The brain scans and profiling these Erosians did obviously went far deeper than what kind of sex toys someone liked.

"I admit," she said slowly, "that your rather dominant behavior since I've arrived has been very exciting. I mean, you're right, I'm not used to anyone telling me what to do, or 'forcing' me to do it. I'm certainly not used to having my bottom spanked!"

She blushed a little, recalling how the sting of the spanking had somehow transmuted itself into sexual heat inside of her. She recalled the intense orgasm of the night before, and that was only his fingers and tongue! What would his cock be like?

Remembering that he could hear her thoughts as if she spoke them aloud, she felt the heat creep up her cheeks, but Ronan only smiled slightly. "Go on," he encouraged. "Share with me. What was it like to be held by the force field, unable to stop me, whatever I chose to do?"

"It was," she stopped, searching for the words. "It was exhilarating. Yes, it really was! To know that I couldn't get away from you, no matter what you did, was very arousing for some reason. I felt so feminine, so sexy, so desired. It was," now she grinned, seeing his point, "freeing."

"That's perfect!" Ronan said. "Because today we are going to work further with that idea. From my studies of human behaviors, and my own human impulses when I am in this form, I have deduced that in order for a human to fully submit, with grace and honesty, he or she needs to trust the person involved. While it's sexy and exciting for me to 'demand' that you submit, it only works on a deeper level if that is what you truly wish to do. You need to be willing to 'let go' and to do that, you have to trust.

"I know it's a lot to ask, that you trust me so soon after we have met. But perhaps because of the nature of our liaison and our very short time together, you will be able to suspend the usual courtship rituals and time involved and take that leap of faith with me."

She looked at him, at the long lean planes of his face, his eyes like liquid gold and full of fire. Did he burn for her? The turn of his body toward her, the way he had held her in the night, the way he now seemed so eager to teach her, to help her discover her own sensual secrets... Was this all just part of the package? Or was there something more between them? Was it going to be reciprocal? Was this even permitted?

He didn't respond to her unspoken thoughts, perhaps respecting that she hadn't voiced them. His hand, still covering hers, moved slowly up her arm, his fingers lightly touching her skin, sending little jolts of desire through her as they moved up to her shoulder, to her throat and down to her breast, partially exposed in her silken robe.

"What did you have in mind?" she whispered.

"I'll show you."

Chapter Four

Aria was naked, standing in the center of the room. Ronan stood next to her, a long red sash in his hands. "I'm going to bind you, my love. Slowly. The bondage itself is part of the experience. Part of your willingness to trust me as you lose control, slowly, of each part of your body."

Aria wrapped her arms protectively around herself. Yes, she wanted this, but at the same time, she was afraid. Ronan gently took her hands, pulling them so that her arms rested loosely at her sides. He kissed her forehead and whispered, "Be at peace, little Aria. I will not take you further than you wish to go. You control the process, though I will control you and your actions. You see the lovely symmetry of it, do you not?"

Aria wasn't sure what he was talking about but his tone was soothing and kind, and she relaxed, deciding to trust him as best she was able. Ronan nodded, accepting her silent acquiescence.

"First," he said, "I'm going to blindfold you. This is a way to release you from one form of control. You don't have to be constantly vigilant about what you think is going to happen next." As he spoke, he lifted her heavy mane of silvered hair from her neck, carefully securing the crimson sash beneath it. He checked it, satisfied that she could not see.

"Now I'm going to bind your hands behind you. I want you to feel the rope. To experience the fact that you can no longer use your hands or arms. Not to defend yourself, or protect yourself, or even to balance. You will give all that to me."

He took her arms, aware of the slight tremble, and gently moved them behind her. Using a silky blood-red rope of some strong material much like nylon, he wound it several times just above her elbows, forcing her arms up high behind her, causing her breasts to jut out as she arched her back to accommodate the rope.

Next, he bound her wrists. Still using the same piece of rope, he brought it around her torso, above the breasts and then below, winding it and using the ends to cinch it tightly together on each side.

Aria swayed a little and he steadied her, drawing her into his arms for a moment and nuzzling her neck. "You are doing beautifully," he assured her. She did not reply, but her breathing was becoming ragged. Ronan dropped a hand down to her sex, touching the hot folds. He felt her moisture and sensed her obvious arousal.

For a moment he teased her, massaging her pussy until she moaned and shifted, trying to get his hand more firmly upon her. Laughing a little, he said, "Oh no, not yet, my love. Not yet. You will feel the bite of rope before you enjoy the kiss of love. And we're only halfway there."

Ronan wrapped several more feet of rope around Aria's slender waist. Looping it around the belt of rope, he brought it down between her legs, wrapping it in a similar loop at her back. He pulled it tight, cinching it so that the rope pulled tightly against her sex, burying itself between her labia and pressing hard against her clit.

Aria moaned, spreading her legs to try and relieve some of the pressure against her tender sex. "Oh," Ronan said, feigning innocence though his eyes were blazing, and his cock was straining eagerly in his pants, "Do you want to spread your legs? I can help with that. In fact, I'll do better. We're going to spread those gorgeous legs of yours wide, my slave girl. We're going to suspend them from the ceiling. You will be completely immobilized and entirely at my mercy."

It took a moment for his words to register. The rope was tight against her pussy, and she felt her own hot juices seeping around it. She hadn't expected such a strong physical reaction to being bound so tightly, her arms almost uncomfortably tight behind her back, her breasts outlined by rope above and below. Then his words penetrated. Suspended from the ceiling?! That was going too far!

"No," she said, and it came out as a hoarse whisper. Yet even as she protested, her pussy responded to the image it produced in her brain, of her naked body, covered in rope, legs spread wide, dangling from the ceiling like an offering, like a sacrifice to some ancient erotic god.

Ronan understood that her voiced "no" was from fear, but that her curiosity and desire outweighed that fear. Taking her in his strong arms, he gently lowered her to the floor, until she was resting, somewhat awkwardly because of the ropes, on her side.

She felt him slip something thick and soft around each ankle, and assumed they must be cuffs of some kind. She heard the clink of chain as he attached something to each cuff. "I could use the force field and hold you that way. But the experience will be heightened by the actual force of gravity, pulling at your chains, dragging at the ropes that bind you."

Ronan attached the chains to a device in the ceiling that was revealed when he pushed a button on a panel set inconspicuously in the wall. He pressed another button and slowly, Aria was lifted by the ankles by some kind of magnetic laser field.

She gasped as she felt her body being lifted. The movement was slow and easy, but inexorable. Soon she was suspended, upside down and blindfolded, her arms pinned behind her. Ronan pushed another button, holding it down as Aria's legs were slowly spread by the machine. He let the button go just as she was about to cry to him that it was too much. Her muscles were now strained as her legs were spread as wide as was barely tolerable. Ronan could clearly see the crimson ropes cruelly spreading her labia.

"You belong to me, Aria. You are completely helpless now and under my control. If I wished, I could leave you here, for hours, for days and you could do nothing to protest. If I choose, I can gag your mouth. I can stuff your mouth with my cock. I can choke you with my come. Shall I do that, slave girl? Shall I treat you like an object, to be debased and humiliated?"

Stunned at his language, Aria could only weakly shake her head. Her body was trembling and she no longer knew if it was fear, or desire, or some heady combination of the two. She did want his cock, but not in her mouth. She wanted to feel it fill her. To claim her in that primal way.

The blood was rushing to her head and she felt dizzy. She struggled a moment, trying to lift her head or move her arms, but she only succeeded in swaying a little.

"Please," she whispered, not even sure herself what she was entreating.

She felt Ronan's strong hands upon her, rolling her nipples in his fingers. She heard him kneel next to her, and suddenly his voice was in her ear. "Are you ready to submit, slave girl?"

"To what?" she managed.

"Ah, then you are not. When you are ready, you do not ask to what. You simply acknowledge that you are mine to do with as I will. Do you understand?"

She didn't respond and suddenly she felt a tug against her sex. Ronan was twisting the ropes in such a way that they cinched even tighter, drawing a cry from the bound woman. The rope burned her, and at the same time lit a fire of need so urgent she felt she could come just from its friction.

Ronan teased her this way for several minutes, alternately sliding the rope against her increasingly wet pussy and ratcheting it tightly so that she cried out in pain. It hurt, yes, it actually did hurt, and yet at the same time, it was wonderful! It was beyond arousal for her. She had moved somehow onto another plane, where pleasure and pain truly combined into something more fierce, more present, more real, than simply one or the other.

This time, when Ronan whispered his question, Aria only nodded, eager for whatever he chose to do. She was no longer thinking, but operating purely on instinct and lust. She felt herself being slowly lowered, until her head touched the floor. Ronan was there then, easing her bound body down.

He released the cuffs from her ankles and eased her to her side, so she was not pinning down her own arms beneath her. Deftly he untied the knots at her waist, pulling away the dark red rope, now slick in the spot where it had gripped her sex.

Ronan removed the sash from her eyes, softly covering them with his hand for a moment as she adjusted to the light of the room. Gently he pushed tendrils of hair from her face. "I want to make love to you, Aria. I want you to accept me while you are bound. My slave girl, bound in ropes, while I claim you. Are you freely enslaved now, my love? Do you want this? Do you crave it?"

Aria flushed, but her eyes were bright with desire. She licked her lips, which felt dry. Her skin was hot. Slowly she nodded her head, her eyes locked on his. Ronan stood, at last removing his pants, revealing his large perfect penis, rigid with desire for the bound and naked woman.

He helped her to her feet and brought her to a stool that was the perfect height to bend her over. A gentle kick to her ankles forced her to spread her legs, and he leaned over her, pressing his chest against her bound arms. Reaching around, he grabbed her by the throat, holding her just tightly enough to set her to breathing raggedly. She knew this wasn't real. She wasn't being held by the throat and raped, while helplessly bound and miles from any help. No, this was completely consensual. And yet, her body was responding as if she was two people or had two desires raging at once within her.

One part of her didn't perceive that it was a game. This part forced adrenaline to course madly, zigging and zagging through her veins, readying her to fight or flee. It made her heart pump erratically and all her nerve endings were at attention.

But another part was liquid desire, raging heat. She wanted him to take her, just like this. Tied up, pussy aching and soaked with her own juices. She could smell the scent of her arousal in the air. She was reduced to pure, raw sex. She didn't just want him to fuck her at last. She was desperate for it. And just like this. Bent over the stool, like a slut in heat, existing only for his cock.

She grunted in animal pleasure as he pressed his erect organ against her. She was so ready that he slipped in, filling her completely. It was like nothing she had ever experienced. Aria was used to being on top, literally and figuratively. When she made love with men, she generally preferred to ride them like stallions, using their bodies to please her own. She was always assured of an orgasm because she could control the friction of their bodies against her clit.

They would also come, watching her astride them, her long silver hair streaming behind her as she lost herself in her selfish pleasures. She realized suddenly that she had never made love to a man. She had engaged in mutual masturbation, each partner using the other, even pleasing the other, but with some crucial element missing.

Her thoughts were obliterated as Ronan entered her fully and began a slow, sensual dance, rotating his hips seductively as he pressed deeply into her. Aria moaned with pleasure, the ropes biting into her arms and wrists only enhancing her masochistic pleasure.

When Ronan came inside of her, calling her name in a fierce cry, she arched back into him, longing to take him even deeper, to keep him there forever. Soon, however, Ronan pulled away, leaving Aria bent and sprawled over the stool. She felt too weak even to move, though her pussy was still on fire and she hadn't climaxed.

She felt Ronan's arms around her as he lifted her from the stool, and then took her in his arms, carrying her to the soft bed. "Shall I untie you?" he asked.

"That is for you to say, Sir," she whispered, though even as she spoke these submissive words they surprised her.

"Ah, that is different then," Ronan replied, his eyes dancing. "Then I shall leave you bound just a while longer. I do like to see a bound woman orgasm." He activated the bed's force field and Aria felt her body lifting again into the air, though this time it defied gravity.

With her arms bound tight beneath her, she was completely helpless as Ronan leaned over her, licking against her swollen and now sticky sex. "You are burning up," he murmured, as he gripped her thighs, holding her open so he could kiss and lightly bite her spread and swollen sex.

Arousal and exhaustion combined to send her quickly over the edge of an intense and sweet release. "Oh, oh, oh!" she cried in a little voice as his tongue played its lovely rhythm on her sex.

While she was still suspended, Ronan quickly undid the knots at her sides and unwound the ropes from her torso and arms. He lay beneath her, receiving her as she was lowered by the diminishing force field.

He gently massaged her limbs. The blood sent a stinging pain through her arms and hands as it returned to full flow. Aria was like a rag doll, limp from exertion and soaked in sexual satisfaction.

"Are you happy?" he whispered. But there was no answer.

Aria was fast asleep.

Chapter Five

It was Aria's third day on the planet. In some respects, the time was flying, in others it was as if she'd always been here. She had risen late and fancied a swim and perhaps a picnic on the beach. Ronan had other ideas.

"Now we will begin your training for this evening."

"Training! This is a sex spa, not a health club. What are you talking about?"

"Tonight you dance for the senior council. You are the entertainment."

"I'm the *what*?!" Aria's eyes flashed with indignation. What was this impudent man talking about! Even as she thought this, the image of the lovely dancers of Iris Nine flashed through her mind. The highly trained belly dancers were considered the premiere seductresses of the Andromeda Galaxy. They were actually slaves, stolen by the Iris Nine traders from throughout the galaxy and selected based on their grace and beauty. But they were slaves only in that they were not free to leave. They were treated as queens while they resided on the planet. The ultimate goal was their purchase, and its consummation had to be two ways. Only if the Iris Nine dancer accepted the bidder was he or she free to take them.

The dancers were famous for their evocative use of scarves as they danced, simulating sexual acts that made their audience literally spring to attention.

Aria had always harbored a secret admiration for these women, idly dreaming that she might dance like that, if she weren't so busy running corporations and jetting around the galaxy. Of course! Ronan had pulled yet another fantasy out of her mind. It was disconcerting!

"I want a block. I want a mind block," she now said. She knew there were telepathic species who used these blocks as a courtesy, a way of staying out of the minds of strangers. Surely, such a thing existed on Eros.

"It's good to want things," Ronan said, grinning. "But I'm afraid such a device wouldn't be a good idea for you. You spend enough of your time blocking out things, staying focused, moving in a straight line to your goal."

As he spoke, Ronan pushed a panel with his foot and the wall, which had been a pleasing soft blue, now turned transparent, revealing the glorious summer's day, with white sand and green ocean and yellow birds wheeling overhead against the sunlit sky. Aria stared at the gorgeous view, forgetting for a moment her protests.

Ronan continued, "Take a moment. Breathe. This is your week. Hand it over to me. I will punish you again, dear, if you deserve it. You aren't the CEO here. Not with me. You are my love slave. Mine. To do with as I please.

"And it pleases me to have you dance tonight. Your body is supple. You should have no trouble learning the basic moves. You have a natural grace. And we'll use a training cap which should dramatically decrease your learning time."

Training caps had been in wide use for some time, but improvements were constant and exponential. An entire university education could be assimilated in a matter of hours by wearing the cap, which directly downloaded relevant information to the brain. Aria had always regarded such devices as "cheating". The drawback was that you learned precisely what someone else had programmed, with their particular spin on that knowledge. Still, it had its uses, she was willing to admit, such as when she had forgotten about an important meeting with a new client, and yet was able to learn all the salient details about their product line and philosophies in a matter of minutes.

"You'd have me parading in front of a bunch of men like some Iris Nine slave woman?" Aria's tone was indignant.

"Very much like that, yes. Although it won't be your job to seduce the people watching you. And you won't be sold to the highest bidder, as the slaves of Iris Nine are." He smiled. As he stood from the table, Aria tried not to stare at his bare, smooth chest and firm stomach. "Let me show you what you'll be wearing."

He produced a lovely gown of sheer gossamer pink. It was streaked with silver and white, so that it looked almost animate. He also showed her the long scarves she would be using in the graceful dances. Aria's protests were momentarily stilled by the beautiful clothing. She did adore a lovely gown, and she recognized the superior craftsmanship and cut of this one.

"It was designed especially for you, Aria. You should be ravishing in it. Would you like to try it on?" Aria was wearing the soft robe he had left for her on her bed. She stood now, eager to put on the beautiful things.

Ronan assisted her, and for some reason she didn't feel shy in front of him, though she was again naked. Perhaps her body's memory of his searing kisses had allowed the mantle of modesty to fall.

The gown fit perfectly. The shimmering fabric cupped her breasts softly, lifting and pressing them together like ripe fruit offered on a plate. The folds of the special material clung alluringly to her lithe shape, creating an erotic effect more enticing than if she was nude. Aria twirled delightedly, admiring herself in a mirror on the wall.

Laughing, Ronan handed her the long scarves she would need for her dance. "I told you, you were a natural." Carefully he placed the training cap on her head, pressing it so the necessary contact could be established. Aria stilled as data downloading from the dance routines was programmed into her brain.

At length Ronan removed the cap from her head. Taking the little silver flute that had led her to him that first evening, Ronan sat lightly on a stool and began to play a haunting melody.

Pausing for a moment, he said, "Dance," and Aria obeyed. Her body began undulating effortlessly, like grace personified. Her face was lax, almost as if she were in a trance, but in fact she was highly alert. It was novel to feel her body executing flawless moves that she had no idea she knew. Indeed, she hadn't known them a moment before, but now she glided and circled around Ronan like a seasoned Iris Nine dancer.

The music seemed to guide her, or she guided it, she wasn't sure. After a few moments, she and the music were weaving together in a complex tapestry of artistic but highly sexual expression. Every fiber of her being seemed somehow more alive, more sensual than she could ever remember experiencing. A sexual power was emanating from her in a lovely, steady pulse of desire. And yet, there was something spiritual in the connection—something loftier than mere sexual desire. She felt as if she were part of some sacred feminine expression of beauty and poetry.

Ronan continued to play, his eyes riveted on the beautiful dancing woman. Aria now saw his penis, rising hard and clearly outlined against the soft linen of his pants. She smiled slightly as her body twisted and swayed, forcing her to use muscles she hadn't even known she possessed.

After about thirty minutes, Aria collapsed exhausted on a couch. She was bathed in a sheen of sweat and breathing hard. "That's a workout!" she exclaimed. She didn't add that it had been something more than that. He knew, of course, if he looked into her thoughts, that she had been moved by the experience in a way she hadn't expected. For now, she wasn't willing to articulate it.

"You were phenomenal, Aria. You will turn heads tonight, I can assure you!"

"Not just heads, it seems," she said, grinning in the direction of his cock, which was still evident in the linen pants.

Ignoring the jibe, Ronan said, "I bet you could use a swim in the ocean about now. Let's test the waters, shall we? I think you'll find the temperature to your liking. The sun will be too hot later in the day, but right now it's perfect. Shall we?"

The thought of cool, refreshing waves splashing over her heated body sounded perfect. "Let's go!" Ronan helped Aria to remove the dancing gown. He told her it would be clean and fresh for her this evening, but for now he just dropped it on the sofa, leaving her standing naked before him.

While she watched, he stepped out of his own pants, revealing himself completely before her. His body was that of a mythical god and Aria gazed appreciatively at him, her mouth actually watering. Nudity was common on most planets and the beaches of New Earth were almost all nude beaches. One had to seek out the more modest areas, if one was so inclined.

Aria, proud of her own body, always went to the nude beaches and so wasn't surprised when Ronan stripped in anticipation of their swim. He was quite a sight, with his long, lean muscles, and the well-formed penis rising to attention from its nest of pubic curls. The lovely memory of it buried inside her to the hilt made her literally squirm. Ronan grinned at her, but said nothing.

He extended a hand and she took it, letting him lead her. He picked up a large duffel bag he must have prepared earlier and they left the cozy little house together. The sun was bright, almost too hot already for Aria's skin but the water, as Ronan had promised, was perfect. The waves frothed and foamed against Aria's toes, then rose to her ankles. Together they waded, walking deeper into the waves, until finally she summoned the courage to dive headlong into one. Soon she was swimming up through it like a little seal, tossing back her silver curls, now gleaming wetly in the sunlight.

Ronan leaped in as well, swimming strongly alongside her until they both tired and returned dripping to the sand. Ronan spread out a large soft towel and opened a tall thin tent-like shelter, which blocked the sun, but still let the soft wind blow gently over them.

As Aria lay back, Ronan smoothed a soft unguent into her skin, moving his long fingers deftly over her body. Aria sighed with pleasure, letting her eyes close as she inhaled the citrus scent of the ointment coupled with the salty tang of the sea.

Ronan paused at her breasts, kneading them softly, and then lightly pinching her nipples until they were fully erect. Aria moaned softly and shifted, feeling the sweet wetness begin in her center. She wished his hands would go lower, and apparently her wish was acknowledged by the telepath because he slipped his hands down to her sex, gently parting her legs.

Aria's moans became louder as Ronan teased and fondled her pussy, drawing the moisture from her and then entering her with his fingers, first one, then two. Aria half-sat up, reaching for Ronan with her arms, her mouth. He leaned into her, kissing her, twisting her wet hair in his fingers.

She could feel his hard body against hers, cool now as the water evaporated. His cock was hard against her thigh as he pulled her up close to him. They kissed for several minutes until Aria pulled away, her face flushed, her breathing labored.

Lips parted, Aria stared hungrily at Ronan's straining cock. Ronan's golden eyes darkened with lust as he knelt up, offering his full erection to her attentions. Delicately Aria circled the head of his cock with her tongue, knowing just how to tease him.

Sensually she eased down, taking the head fully into her mouth, savoring its spongy texture and licking the drop of pre-cum at the tip. Bracing herself on her knees, she leaned over and down, taking his full shaft into her throat, and sitting perfectly still for a moment, feeling the pulse of his blood pound in his cock.

With a gentle touch, she cupped his balls, lightly raking them with her fingernails, while her hot mouth clung to him, drawing a cry of pleasure. As she pulled back, she looked up at the man. His head was back, his hair shining golden in the light, the tendons on his neck distended, his face a mask of passion. Though she knew he wasn't in fact human at all, his reactions were certainly those of a human man. At any rate, he was clearly enjoying her attentions.

This was something Aria was used to. She was used to being the one in control, in all aspects of her sexual relationships, and she had perfected her ability to drive a man wild with her mouth and fingers. She knew just when to be soft and delicate, when to increase the pace and intensify the attentions until the man she had chosen burst with pleasure into her mouth. She leaned in now "for the kill", intent on bringing Ronan to a searing orgasm that would render him *her* love slave.

Instead of shuddering and arching into her as she had expected, Ronan pulled away, drawing himself from her until his cock was completely out of her mouth. She opened her eyes, confused. Without speaking, Ronan pressed against Aria's shoulders, forcing her back so that her legs were pinned under her body. When she tried to get back to her knees, he said, "Lie still, little one. You are not in control here."

He held her down with one hand, while the other slowly pumped his own cock, hard and erect in front of her, very close to her face as he leaned over her. She watched, fascinated, as his long, strong fingers moved up the shaft, the thumb pressing down over the head, and then allowing it to peek through as his hand slid down again.

She was mesmerized by the huge penis, which seemed to grow even larger as he massaged it over her. After a few moments, Ronan's head fell back again, his eyes closing. Groaning, he shot his seed across Aria's face and breasts. She sputtered as some of it landed in her mouth.

Outrage mixed with confused lust as Aria lay, naked and spattered with this man's sperm, like some common whore! But the beautiful image of his erect and glorious member, spurting little pearls of jism as his strong, tan body arched back in ecstasy, made her pussy all the wetter. And if she were honest, the very fact of being held down and treated like an object had deeply aroused Aria.

She wanted him, now. *Fuck me*, she thought, *please*! Smiling, Ronan bent down and kissed the girl, wiping his own ejaculate from her face and breasts with a damp cloth he produced from his duffel bag.

Apparently, he didn't share the male human trait of needing a little time to recover. When he pressed his cock against her wet opening, it was as hard as ever. Aria actually squealed with pleasure as he filled her. Her muscles clamped down on his masculine perfection and she wrapped her legs around his hips, pulling him farther into her hot tunnel.

Ronan fucked Aria, pressing deep into her, his hips executing a perfect erotic dance against hers. She knew she could come like this, with his pubic bone thrusting against her clit. She abandoned herself to the pleasure of his actions when, again, she was surprised.

Ronan was standing up, with Aria still in his arms, and his cock still buried in her pussy! Out of instinct, she clung to his neck, afraid of falling. Ronan whispered, "I shall take you in the sea, my love. Just hold onto me and you'll be safe."

He walked the short distance across the sand, which was now hotter from the fully risen sun. The heat of it felt good against Aria's wet hair, and she let her head fall back, feeling the kiss of sun against her cheeks. Ronan held her securely in his arms, as if she weighed no more than a child.

Each step he took caused his cock to glide deeper and then withdraw slightly, a constant tease. Aria found herself clutching his hips tightly with her legs. She wanted that cock to stay just where it was, filling her with pleasure.

The water felt cool against her ass as Ronan took her deeper and deeper into the waves. When the water rose to just below his chest, Ronan stopped. He had taken her past the breaking waves and now swells washed over them on their way to crash against the shore.

Aria's body was half-submerged in the cool salty water, while her face and breasts were warmed by the late morning sun. Still Ronan's rock-hard member was buried inside of her and now he began to undulate and move against her, renewing the lovely friction against her swollen bud.

The combination of sensations—of warm sun, cool water, his strong arms, his cock impaling her—was nothing short of sublime, and Aria was overcome with sheer physical pleasure. She came hard, just a few seconds before Ronan. All the while, he held her safe in his arms, protecting her from the pull of the tides.

She felt his heart pounding and thudding against her own as he recovered himself. Slowly he lifted her away from his body and gently set her down so that she stood next to him in the water. Impulsively Aria reached up and hugged his neck, pulling him down so she could kiss his cheeks, his nose, his chin.

She felt something strange, an emotion she couldn't quite place, welling inside of her. It was almost painful, like an ache in her heart, and yet it was a sweet pain. She didn't yet have a name for it but she hoped whatever it was, it would last.

Chapter Six

Somehow, Aria had imagined that the little blue house with the red roof was all that existed on this continent—at least all that existed for her. But that evening, after a nice dinner of flaky meat pies and fruit sorbet, Ronan had taken Aria to what he called the Meeting House.

After their tryst in the sea, Ronan had brought Aria back to the house for a nap, some more dance practice and some lazy loving in the canopied bed. No force fields were employed and Aria found herself almost wishing for something along those lines. The fantasy of captive slave girl was a powerful one indeed, once she'd acknowledged its existence.

They'd dozed, and then Ronan had slipped out to prepare their meal, while Aria lounged about in a deep tub full of very hot water and sweet scented oils. After dinner, Ronan had attended Aria, more like her servant than her master. He arranged her long silvery hair in series of braids that were traditional for the Iris Nine slave dancers. These braids were designed to move with the dancer, enhancing the effect of the scarves, which were skillfully woven and whipped through the hair as part of the dance.

She again donned the shimmery gown and little silver and white shoes that slipped onto her feet as if they had been custom-made. Indeed, they had been. Aria felt beautiful and sexy. But she also felt something more subtle or perhaps more real. She wasn't certain how to define it. She looked toward Ronan, a question on her face. She realized as she did so that she had taken to speaking less and less as Ronan could read her mind as clearly as he could hear her voice. It was strange to know he could "hear" her thoughts, and yet it was also liberating in some respects.

She was a woman so used to playing her emotions close to the vest, that a part of her had forgotten how to be open about her true feelings. Sometimes they seemed to be hidden even from herself. Yet, with Ronan she found herself curiously free. Was it because this was only for a week? Was it because she knew at the end of that time she would bid him a fond farewell and go back to her life as a driven executive, combing the galaxy for new ideas to earn herself yet more money and power?

Now Ronan answered her, and his response at first took her by surprise. She started to deny it, but then closed her lips. "What you're feeling, Aria, is submission. You're feeling, perhaps for the first time in your life, a desire to submit to another person. You want to please me. You want to obey what I command of you. You want to make me happy."

Ronan's tone was matter of fact, but toward the end of his remarks, something different seemed to enter his voice. As if he too, was just realizing the implications of this and how it made *him* feel. Was there something like awe in his voice? A certain modest pride that this graceful, beautiful woman found something in him that brought out her natural submissive tendency?

As if shaking off an unacceptable idea, Ronan actually shook his own head and said abruptly, "Come. We mustn't keep the Elders waiting."

Now they entered the Meeting House, a small round building built of stone, topped with a golden dome. Aria realized this was the building she had seen that first night. It had intricate carvings of birds and animals around its doors and windows. Inside, the room was warm and inviting, with a large fire leaping against the grate of a massive stone fireplace. Several tables were set near the fire. These were draped with long red cloths and covered with dishes and goblets.

It was clear that a large meal had just been eaten by the Erosians sitting around the tables. Servants were busy removing plates and replenishing wine goblets. Aria noted that though the figures were humanoid, they were definitely not humans. They had the same basic build, with a head, two arms and legs, and a trunk, but their eyes were especially large in their faces and bright golden. Not only the irises but the pupils as well.

Their skin was pale, and their bodies were clothed in long brightly colored robes. Aria realized what was most striking was that they had no hair anywhere to be seen on their bodies. She realized these must be Erosians in their natural form. Ronan himself must look something like this! The thought was unsettling, because it reduced what she thought she had with him. For him, after all, it was only a job, a charade to please the customer. The exterior he had adopted had been pulled from her subconscious. He wasn't real.

She was drawn back to the hall by Ronan's whisper. "These are our Elders. They govern our community. It is an honor to be asked to dance for them. Dance and music are Erosian passions. Perhaps our only passions. The Elders can be difficult to please, but I want you to dance only for me. For me, and for yourself." His tone was warm, even loving. Perhaps his species were all consummate actors.

She sighed, taking in the dozen Erosians sitting at their tables. Their heads were large on long slender necks. The skulls, completely hairless, but covered in supple, pale skin, were beautifully shaped ovals, with their large golden eyes set deep below broad, smooth foreheads. It was impossible to discern gender, at least to her inexperienced eye. They were all dressed in the same robes, differing only in pattern and color. The material looked satiny soft and shimmering in the soft light of the room, which seemed to emanate from the walls. The Elders turned to stare at her and Ronan as they entered the hall.

Ronan took her hand and whispered, "You'll be wonderful. Just be faithful to the music and the dance will take you on its wings. Remember, you are dancing for me."

Bowing before the Elders, Ronan said to them, "May I present Aria, my slave, for your entertainment. You will find her gifted in the ways of the Dance."

With that simple introduction, Ronan led his charge to the center of the room. A large space had been cleared for her dance, leaving only the smooth stone floor, and to the side, a small stool, upon which Ronan now sat.

Aria felt butterflies in her stomach. She was used to making presentations in front of large diverse groups, but she was usually wearing her high-powered executive outfits, with her long hair pulled back in a fashionable but conservative way.

Certainly, she'd never dreamed she'd find herself dressed in gossamer clothing that fit her form like a second skin, revealing every curve and nuance. Even the outline of her nipples was clear against the clinging fabric. As she took in the faces of the assembled group, she saw that they were all staring at her, their features impassive. It might have been her imagination, but they almost seemed to be scowling.

The sound of Ronan's little flute trebled in the air. Aria's body, recently conditioned by the training cap, began to move, despite her nervousness. As she looped and twisted gracefully among the tables, letting the music guide her, she forgot to be nervous.

The dance itself took over, drawing her into its complex patterns and rhythms. The scowls seemed to give way to pure admiration, as everyone in the room, including the servants, stopped whatever they had been doing to give Aria their full attention.

Only sheer exhaustion finally stopped her, and indeed, she might have kept on in spite of it, but Ronan brought the dance to a close with his music, playing a final haunting tune that signaled the end of the ceremonial dance.

Aria sank gracefully to the floor, her head dropping to her chest, still in the thrall of the dance that had taken her over so completely. The room was completely silent. Had this been a real Iris Nine banquet, the bidding would have begun, and, though Aria was unaware of this, she would have drawn quite a high price. She was, as Ronan had assured her, a natural.

Instead of the delicate clinking of little gold hammers on glass, which would have signaled the bids from various species without the necessity of language, the Elders instead turned away from the young woman, nodding amongst themselves, not needing spoken words to convey whatever they might be saying to one another. Her dismissal was evident in their actions.

The spell was broken and Aria lifted her head, looking toward Ronan for direction. She was completely soaked in sweat under the lovely gown and now began to feel cold as it evaporated from her skin. She felt confused, let down somehow. She realized she had been expecting, if not a standing ovation, at least some acknowledgment of her performance by the viewers.

Ronan shook his head at her, very slightly, as if indicating she should remain silent. He stood, pocketing the little flute and leaned down to help Aria to her feet. Together they left the Meeting House, walking in silence the short way back to his home.

Later, sipping a hot, sweet drink from delicately pattern cups, Ronan and Aria nestled in the large canopy bed. Ronan was talking, answering questions both asked and only thought. To him they were the same.

Aria was aware that Ronan was uncomfortable with some of her questions. And yet, he seemed to be trying to answer them honestly. "What you need to understand," he said, when she questioned how indifferent, almost cold the Elders had seemed to her performance, "is that while our industry is primarily based on our recreational spas, sex spas as you call them, there is a certain, uh, disapproval, at high levels."

"How so?"

"Well, our culture still holds vestiges of, what would I call it, prudery. Yes, that's the word. Erosians themselves aren't sexual, and indeed actually frown on an 'overabundance' of sexual activity or desire."

"Sounds like our culture, hundreds of years ago. Lots of illicit sex, but the overall cultural attitude among many communities was that was sex was 'dirty' or 'sinful'. It was tied to ancient religious beliefs that were created to keep the masses under control. Happily, we've abandoned all that nonsense." She blushed a little, suddenly realizing how that must have sounded to Ronan. She was basically condemning what was still very real and prevalent in his own culture.

He laughed a little, of course reading her discomfort. "Please, don't even think to apologize. Though, I should clarify. Unlike your ancient culture, here there is an *absence* of desire. It isn't that it's hidden and then hypocritically condemned. It doesn't even exist."

Aria absorbed this for a moment. Then she said, "But Ronan, isn't it ironic that you make a whole industry out of something, sexual pleasure and hedonism, that your people basically find, if not repugnant, at least distasteful?"

"It is ironic, and yet it makes sense in a way. Because we are so emotionally removed from it, perhaps that is why we are so good at it. We don't succumb to the charms of those we are titillating over the course of the well paid for week. We don't share the same libidinous desires and predilections, and so, when time's up, we say goodbye to the customer and move on to the next job. We are impervious to their requests or demands that the week continue. We know the risks—we've seen them all too often."

Aria's eyes had filled with tears at his callous reminder that she was "just a job". She turned away, trying to hide her feelings, but of course, Ronan could sense them. With a finger, he turned her face back toward his. His expression was gentle.

"Darling girl," he whispered. "Why do you think I share this? I am not like the others. Playing this role, of becoming the sexual fantasy for whoever has the currency to procure me—I find it increasingly difficult. I can't stay neutral, it seems. I think I must have human blood. Because the only time I am truly happy is when I take your human form, and experience your human physical and emotional states of being." He continued, his voice growing excited, "You have no idea the depth of your experience! The range of your emotions, the delicate nuance of your thoughts! Humans are so complex and highly sexual. We Erosians are so different. We are, quite literally, worlds apart."

Clinging to his offering, that he was different, and by inference, that she wasn't merely a customer, Aria urged him to continue. The Erosian culture was generally a secretive one, and she hadn't known much about it, she realized, other than about their famous sex resorts.

"Our people have little use for sex per se. We appreciate the artistic value of a nude form, but there is little sexual interest beyond procreation. Our very sexual organs have changed over the millennia, and now we no longer even have the physical sensation of pleasure to drive us to procreate. It is strictly through our minds and the desire that the species continue, that we have what you would call sex.

"I know for some of us, the chance to assume other forms, and experience their sexual pleasure, makes up for our own rather dry experience. It is exciting and novel to become a Nonian, for example, known for their sexual prowess and six-day orgasms, or to assume the human shape, and the wild and complex emotions that go along with it. I feel so alive when I am human!

"Perhaps that is the key," he said, his voice suddenly softer, as if sharing in his own revelation. "I don't assume a human form, somehow I actually *become* human! The scowls you may have noticed at the Meeting House tonight were not for you, my love, but for *me*. They could read my feelings, of course, and realize I was all too human for good taste or appropriate behavior! I've been reprimanded before, you know. Many times. I've been called before the Elders because I have behaved in too 'human' a fashion for their tastes. I guess I like what I do too much and that grates on them."

"Well, can't you just tell them to go to hell? Start your own resort or something?"

Ronan looked startled, as if such an idea had never occurred to him. "No, no, I could never do that. That would thwart the entire Erosian way. We hold our Elders in the utmost esteem. To break away would be considered the highest treason."

Aria looked at her week-long lover, taking in his lovely features which had been manufactured for her. He looked troubled, even sad. She didn't understand his allegiance to a people from whom he clearly felt alienated, but she knew enough to know that she didn't have to understand something for it to be valid to another.

"Am I just a job?" she whispered, biting her lip as she awaited his answer. Even if it was a lie, she wanted him to say she was more than that.

"Aria," he whispered, "have you heard nothing I've said? How can you ask?" His kiss was the rest of his answer as he claimed her with his mouth.

Chapter Seven

Aria was suspended, face up, a few meters above the bed. Ronan had used the force field to lift her into the air. Her legs were spread at a lewd angle, revealing the little labia and flower bud of her hooded clit. Her arms were spread cruciform and her long silver hair streamed below her.

Aria's eyes were covered again with the red sash. Ronan stood alongside the bed, attaching something to her sex. "I'm going to stimulate you with this device, my love slave, and you are going to control yourself. You are not to orgasm, no matter what I do to you. If you do, I'll punish you. Do you understand?"

The suspended woman nodded. Even though she knew this was just a game, she felt the arousal of being bound in midair, helpless and at this strong man's mercy. Whatever he was pressing against her pussy suddenly jerked into life, emitting a strong current that created a vibration against her clit.

It felt wonderful, and a warm buttery sensation filled Aria's sex, emanating out through her limbs. She knew it wouldn't be long before she came. She remembered his admonition that she mustn't orgasm and said, "Ronan. I'm going to come if you do that! I can't help it! It's a physiological reaction. I can't control it."

Ronan lightly slapped Aria's cheek, making her gasp. "Of course you can control it. You simply have no discipline. You are so used to getting whatever you want, whenever you want it, that you have never even tried to control your orgasm. I'm going to teach you. We begin," he paused, and Aria felt the current increase against her sex, "now."

A moan was wrenched from her lips. She writhed in the air, weightless but held still and spread, unable to close her legs or lower her arms. The pressure against her sex felt like a perfect cock, gliding against her. Her body began to buck and sweat prickled under her arms. "Oh," she gasped. "Please! I can't help it! Please!"

She slipped over the edge of orgasm, squealing with pleasure and release. The buzzing against her sex stopped, and she waited, her heart pounding, knowing she had disobeyed her "master", but feeling too wonderful at the moment to care.

She realized she was waiting for Ronan to speak. Perhaps to remove the blindfold and release the force field. All was silent around her. "Ronan?" she ventured uncertainly. "Are you there? Let me down."

"You have no discipline. You will be punished." His voice was hard. Even though it must be a game, it didn't feel like one just then. She felt him pull away the masturbatory device, but still he didn't let her down.

Aria's heart clutched as she demanded, "Stop it now. This was fun, but now it's not. Let me down."

She felt her head pulled back by her hair. "Who do you think you're talking to, little girl?" Ronan's voice was low and quiet in her ear. Aria gasped as he pulled her hair harder, wrenching her head back. "I told you I would punish you."

She felt herself being flipped over. It was an odd sensation, to be held on pillows of air, yet be unable to move. Now she was face down, still blindfolded, her arms and legs still spread wide. "This is a tool we find quite effective with Erosians who misbehave. It doesn't happen often as we are an obedient people. But every now and again, someone gets out of hand, and they are punished in the public square, using this cane. If wielded effectively, it doesn't cut the skin, but a novice can do real damage."

As he spoke, Ronan removed the blindfold. Aria turned her head, her eyes widening as she took in the long thin cane of some kind of supple material. She recalled the spanking, almost feeling his strong palm smacking her poor bottom. That had been kind of sexy really, but a cane was something else again!

"Surely you're joking!" she insisted, beseeching Ronan with her eyes. "You set an impossible task for me and now you're going to punish me for it! Please, put it down! This is crazy!"

Ronan grinned at her. "You forget, my love. I can see past your words, into your thoughts. I can see past your weak protestations to the deep arousal this cane is causing you. Yes, I see the fear, too. I sense the very real terror you are experiencing. But I also sense the intense arousal—the actual desire to feel the cut of this rod against your tender flesh. You don't want it, but you do want it. You can hide nothing from me."

"No!" Aria yelled, as the cane landed against the soft flesh just where the thigh meets the buttocks. She screamed, and Ronan responded by hitting the same spot on the other side. Two long white lines arose, changing rapidly to dark pink as the blood suffused the area just below the skin.

Ronan leaned over, kissing the very welts he had just so brutally raised. "Are you ready to try again, my love?"

he whispered into the gasping woman's ear. Setting down the cane, his fingers slid to her pussy, which was sopping wet, in spite of her tears.

"Thank me," he whispered. When she didn't respond he added, "Perhaps another few strokes will help you find your tongue."

"No!" Aria yelled, and then her voice subdued, "Thank you, Sir." Her face flushed with anger and confusion as she herself recognized her own arousal at being treated like a common slave.

Ronan laughed softly, his own cock rising in pleasure as he drew the moisture from his captive's pussy, rubbing up to her clit and down again to her entrance in long, slow motions. Aria moaned as the heat of the welts mingled with the lovely pressure of his fingers.

Again, she felt herself teetering on the edge of a climax. "Please," she whispered, "please," unable to articulate the request.

Of course, he knew what she was asking. She didn't need the words, but the human trait to speak was ingrained in her and she continued to beg, now bucking against his skillful fingers, desperate to come.

"Yes," he answered, "you may come, my darling girl. You are so beautiful, little slave." She responded by giving in completely to her pleasure, crying out as her whole body convulsed with an intense orgasm.

Her heart pounded, then slowly eased, and she found that she could move her limbs. She reached out to Ronan who took her in his arms and gently lowered her to the soft bed. He kissed her forehead, smoothing away the tangled hair, his touch light, but his golden eyes smoldering. The mattress wrapped its form around her, holding her like a babe in its mother's arms, and she slept.

Ronan stood beside the sleeping woman for a quite a while, his expression inscrutable, his hands clenched. At last, he turned away.

Aria awoke to the sound of Ronan's flute, playing a melancholy, mournful tune. She tested her limbs, no force field. Slowly she climbed out of the bed, stretching languorously, her long silver hair glowing against the soft light from the window.

As she caught sight of her reflection in a mirror, Aria smiled, realizing this was the first time in too long to recall that she wasn't rushing off to meetings all over the galaxy or busily planning her schedule, coordinating with her three assistants on the projects of the day. She felt—she had to pause to consider what it was—happy!

Ronan, whom she'd only known a few days, had come to completely fill her consciousness. She realized with a sudden jolt that her feelings for him felt dangerously real. And yet she knew that could only lead to broken dreams. This was, after all, Pleasure Planet.

She recalled the contract she had signed, swearing not to hold the spa liable if she felt feelings other than simple pleasure, once the week was over. She'd signed numerous forms that all basically contained the same message—once your week is up, you leave Eros and that is that. Love certainly didn't enter their equation! This was a job.

And as exciting and romantic a lover as Ronan had proved to be thus far, she realized she had better face the fact that he too was just doing his job. The fact that he did it extraordinarily well didn't give her cause to think this meant anything at all to him.

Even if his "confessions", if that's what they were, about his very real feelings for humans and his pleasure in holding a human form were real, what did it ultimately have to do with her? He had also emphasized what an obedient race the Erosians were and how he dared not offend the authorities.

Sighing, she shook back her hair and took the silky robe he'd again left for her. It clung prettily to her naked body, accenting her long curves and the round lushness of her breasts. When she entered the living room, she found Ronan perched on a high stool, the little silver flute at his lips. He played a few more measures before putting it down and turning slowly toward her.

"Are you refreshed?" he asked. He was again shirtless, wearing only the loose linen pants he seemed to favor. His bare feet gripped the bar of the stool.

"Yes, thank you," she answered. "Your music. It sounded so sad."

"I suppose I am sad," he responded.

"But why?" Sudden insecurities about her own presence there—perhaps she was taking him from his lover or wife, perhaps this job was tedious. She flushed, angry at herself for such weak thoughts. She was Aria Loran after all!

Ronan smiled slowly. She flushed even darker as she realized he was reading her thoughts as clearly as if she had shouted them.

"No lover," he said. "No wife. We don't take permanent mates here. And in fact, your fears, though charming in their vulnerability, have no basis in reality."

He paused, looking out to the crashing sea. "In fact, the opposite is true. You know," he said, turning toward Aria, "when we met, I told you that you could call me Ronan. But that isn't my name."

"Really! Are Erosian names secret or something? Or not to be shared with the tourists?" She tried to keep her tone light but a trace of bitterness crept in.

"No, in fact, we don't have names. We have numbers. The Review Board automatically assigns a number, which has significance if you know how to decipher it. My number is 134256338. If you know how to interpret it, that tells you who my birth parents were, which sector and division I reside in when not working at the spa and certain details about my health record."

"That's fascinating," Aria said sincerely. She always enjoyed learning about new cultures and species. And yet, at the same time, it was disconcerting to think that the very human man she had come to think of as Ronan, to care for as Ronan, was in fact Erosian 134256338.

"Aria! Please forgive me!" Of course, he had heard her thoughts. "I apologize. I have seriously overstepped the boundaries of our relationship. It's not your fault, of course, but," he paused, seeming to look for the right words, "there's something about you. About us. I feel as if we've known each other all our lives. As if our lives were meant to intertwine somehow. I feel as if I truly own you. This is no longer a game, my little slave girl."

He laughed a little, looking embarrassed and admitted, "You know, I could be severely punished for this breach. Our code clearly states what is permitted to be shared with the, uh, tourists, and the details of our sexual and social order certainly aren't among them! And yet, with you, I feel safe, somehow. Even compelled, if you will, to share.

To let you know a little bit about *me* and not just the image I've created to please your eye.

"I know it's ridiculous. Soon our time together will be over and you will be gone. That is why I am sad, I suppose." He stood slowly, pocketing his little flute.

Aria didn't know what to say. She sensed something odd was happening here, perhaps unprecedented, and yet she had to admit she too felt that special connection. It excited her, but it also frightened her.

Ronan brought Aria a tall glass of something cool and refreshing. They sat together on one of the deep couches, enjoying the view of the sea through the clear wall of the abode. The sun was setting like fire over the water, dazzling the eyes. Glittering shades of silver and gold edged the waves. Aria sensed Ronan had more to say, but she decided to let him say it in his own time. She sat silently musing on what was going on between them, on so many different levels.

Oh, the exciting sex, the games of Master and slave, and the entire lush, luxurious experience were certainly part of the "package deal". But what could possibly come of his protestations of love, if that's what they were? As he had pointed out, the week would end soon and that would be that.

Quietly he began to speak. "Aria. I've been working for the spa all my adult life. For many years, it was truly just a job. I would assume the form of the species in question, connect with their inner desires and serve them. I was never involved on any level that mattered to me.

"But over the past few years, especially when humans are involved, it has become more difficult. Too often, it has shaken me, left me somehow different when the experience is over. It's almost as if some protective shield has been breached, and human emotions and needs are seeping into my essence.

"In fact, I put in for a transfer to something in administration, because I find I am having difficulty keeping my Erosian nature intact when inhabiting other life forms, most especially the human body.

"The orders are being processed, and I've been told you will be my last assignment. After this, I am supposed to work behind the scenes, setting up the schedules, taking care of the myriad of details that go into creating these weeks of 'paradise' for species from all over the galaxy. I am not to have further contact with alien species.

"The odd thing is, at first I was relieved when they told me the transfer had come through. I have had far too much trouble controlling my human feelings when I inhabit this human form. I have been reprimanded on several occasions for 'going too far' in my behaviors and, more importantly, my feelings."

"Your feelings! But whose business are those? Who would know?"

"Oh, they know. We are closely monitored. In addition to our regular telepathic natures, we have a chip implanted at birth. All thoughts and feelings are carefully screened by the Review Board. This is essential in the work that we do, to keep our true selves intact while we assume the forms of alien species. I have always accepted that. It's a part of our culture, though I appreciate that to your way of thinking, it is a very 'un-human' sort of intervention. It's really for our own protection.

"And in general I've been able to control myself. It is only with the human form that I seem to have trouble now.

I almost feel more at home in this human skin than in my own hairless, sexless Erosian body. Something's changed. I can't seem to shut it all down now, to compartmentalize these alien feelings and then flush them away when the week is over. And lately, my feelings are bordering on subversive. And it's your fault, my love."

"*My* fault?!" Arias' eyes widened in confusion. "What did I do?"

He smiled, his eyes crinkling kindly, though they shone with sorrow. "You came into my life, little one. You burst in here, with your silver hair, your fiery eyes, your strength of will and your deep submissive sexual streak, and," he dropped his voice to a whisper, "you have captured my heart. I'm in love with you, Aria. And that is forbidden."

Aria stared at him, speechless. Suddenly Ronan stiffened. "I sense them nearby," he said, his expression tense, alert. Lowering his voice to a whisper he continued, "They have been monitoring me! I should have known this would happen. They've come for me. Listen," he took Aria's face in his large hands, cupping it gently. His golden eyes looked almost fierce as he said earnestly, "they may take me from you now. I've let down my guard. I've let my human emotions cloud my judgment. Take these words to heart, Aria. I will come for you! No matter what happens, wait for me and I will come. You will not leave this planet without me, my darling."

"But—" Aria interjected, "they're taking you? Who's taking you? From me? They can't!"

"They can. Read your contract. Forgive me for all of this. I had never planned for love to enter the equation. I was content that this would be my last 'adventure' before I retired to a quiet life of bureaucracy. But you've made it impossible."

Aria started to speak again, but Ronan put his fingers to her lips. "They'll be here in a moment. We must answer their summons. Just tell me this, do you want me to come for you? Do you want to commit yourself to me? If you say no, I will go and we will never see one another again. But if you say yes," he bent and kissed her, his lips searing hers with passion, "if you say yes, my love, I will find you. I will come for you."

"Yes," Aria said, her eyes filling tears, still confused as to what was actually happening.

Ronan stood, pulling Aria up with him. Speaking quickly he said, "Whoever they send as my replacement— you must accept him. Don't let them see that it matters. This will assuage their fears that we are connected by more than a contract."

He stopped a moment, and Aria felt tears overflowing, though she knew she had to remain strong as Ronan wanted. He took her hand, squeezing it reassuringly and said, "Now remember, whoever takes my place, for I am sure now that is what they intend, do what he asks of you and enjoy the few days until we meet again. Give yourself to him as if he were me." Aria started to protest, and of course, Ronan could read her jumbled thoughts and sense her desire to be true to him.

He smiled reassuringly and said, "Jealousy is not a human trait I have much use for, little one. You will be doing this for *me*. For *us*."

"But Ronan! How? They'll know. They'll look in my mind and read it all there as plain as day. They'll know my heart belongs..." she trailed off, suddenly shy, feeling heat bloom on her cheeks. Never before had a man, not since her first love, affected her as this one did. And now he was to be taken from her.

"No, I can give you a mind block. A shield. Many humans find it disconcerting when we peer into their heads and they insist that we stop."

"But you said before—"

He cut her off, smiling sardonically, "It wasn't what you truly wanted, dear heart. In truth, which you will acknowledge if you are honest with yourself, you loved the fact that I could see into your dreams, into your heart. It freed you from having to defend yourself. From having to always maintain that powerful façade that you show to all the worlds."

Aria gasped, silenced by this admission, its truth resonating within her. Ronan sat up again, looking toward the door. "We only have a minute or so. Close your eyes and sit still a moment. I will give you the mind block. They will sense it at once and not attempt to penetrate your thoughts. You won't be at a disadvantage, at least in that regard."

Aria closed her eyes and Ronan closed his as well, placing his hands on her temples. After a moment he said, "It is done."

There was a knock at the door.

Chapter Eight

Aria had expected to see a group of Elders such as had been in attendance when she danced at the Meeting House or some kind of armed guards. She was half-prepared for them to be carrying handcuffs or the "punishment cane", ready to escort Ronan to Erosian Thought Prison for his subversive feelings!

She'd barely had time to process what he had been telling her. The admission of his love for her she stored like a little pearl in her consciousness, to take out and savor when it was safe to do so. For now she steeled herself, ready to fight to protect her man.

But instead of aliens, armed or otherwise, another human being stood outside the door when Ronan opened it. Ronan squeezed Aria's hand reassuringly and whispered, "Remember my promise." A man entered the room, smiling at the two of them. He was breathtakingly handsome, a fact that Aria couldn't help but notice. His long dark hair gleamed blue-black in the fading sunlight, and his features were strong and even, from his high forehead to his firm jaw. Aria realized with a sudden jolt that he was the spitting image of the cover from a romance novel she had read on the ship flight here! Only the golden eyes betrayed him.

Unlike the complex memories and dreams that had allowed them to create Ronan's human shape for her, based on her first true love, this man had clearly been "thrown together", grabbing the first image, closest to the surface of her subconscious. He stood now, tall and strong, muscles brimming against his white shirt, his sizable endowment clearly outlined in black close-fitting pants. He was sexy, in a romance novel kind of way.

But he wasn't Ronan, and Aria found herself curiously disturbed at how they were able to take images from her brain like this and manipulate her feelings as a result. It had been well and good when she'd signed up for it, but this change of events had unnerved her. All these thoughts tumbled over themselves as she tried to come to grips with her bizarre new situation. "Ronan," he said heartily, his voice deep and masculine. "You've been called away on very important business. It can't wait. I have been given the privilege of tending your slave girl in your absence. And from the look of her, I'd say it's a very high privilege indeed! Girl!" He turned his attentions to Aria. "Let's see your form. Strip!"

Aria was reminded of her first night with Ronan. Of her shock, and secret arousal at his insistence that she strip and submit to his attentions. This man was following the same formula, it appeared, reading in her psyche that this behavior excited her and would provide her with pleasure.

She turned to Ronan, uncertain, unwilling to obey this new "master". "Not very obedient, is she, Ronan?" The man chuckled. "Perhaps it's because I failed to observe the human ritual greeting. Please introduce us, Ronan."

Ronan moved forward and said, "Aria, this is Mordan. He will be your pleasure guide for the rest of the week. My apologies on the short notice. You are to obey Mordan in all things, or pay the price. Am I clear?" Mordan grinned, nodding his agreement.

Aria started to object, but Ronan's urgent words were branded in her mind. She was certain what was now happening wasn't part of any scripted role-playing. She and Ronan were engaged in a secret battle for survival — the survival of their fledgling love.

Ronan interrupted her thoughts. His voice sounded formal, almost distant. "It's been a pleasure serving you. I take my leave with your beauty imprinted upon my heart." He bowed low, gave a nod to Mordan and was gone.

Aria stared at the closed door, momentarily stunned. Yes, he had warned her that this would happen but now that it had, and so suddenly, she felt winded as if she'd been punched in the stomach. Ronan was gone. She wanted him back! Her whole being seemed to scream this one thought. Suddenly she whipped about to face the hulking, handsome man before her. Had he read her thoughts?

She let out a little breath of relief, as Mordan simply stood staring impassively at her, his impossibly red lips curled into a devilish smile. "Not used to being handed over, eh?" he said, leering toward her. Her first impulse was to slap his face. How dare he assume she was some actual slave girl, eager to be used by whatever good-looking man happened to be handy? She started to retort, forgetting already Ronan's admonitions to "go along" with things.

But Mordan interrupted, "Please calm your mind, dear lady," his voice soothing. "Perhaps I was hasty in my command that you disrobe. This must be a shock, this sudden change of partners. It is rare, but if you read your contract carefully, you will see in clause 27B, subsection 24, that it does occur and doesn't void the contract per se."

Aria just stared at him, saying nothing. She didn't know exactly what she was feeling, her thoughts were still spinning around the man who was no longer there. She felt suddenly as if she was part of some kind of spy story — an agent with a secret mission. The image empowered her somehow and she stood a little taller, facing her assigned "lover".

"Let's have some tea, and then we shall get to know one another better," Mordan said, taking her arm. He led her to the table, moving about busily as he prepared the food and drink. At last, he sat down, setting out a pretty arrangement of little cakes and tarts as he poured a fragrant hot tea into a ceramic cup.

Holding it out to her he said, "Your reputation precedes you, did you know that, Aria? I have heard talk already about your splendid dance at the Member House. Perhaps I shall require a command performance later on."

Aria smiled a little. For a moment, she felt a small, surging pride at his compliment. Then her mind clouded again, as she saw Ronan, his eyes ablaze with lust and possessive pride as she moved and writhed in tantalizing circles around him.

She considered screaming, demanding a refund, insisting on seeing the Elders to make her case. She considered using her considerable clout and power in the Unified Planetary System to demand the return of Ronan at once! Somehow, she doubted if that power would hold sway here. She knew it would be useless to stamp her feet and wave her fists. Almost as if he were speaking aloud to her, she heard Ronan's words, entreating her to wait for him. He would come for her. Aria, who had never fully trusted a man before, not in ways of the heart, found that she did trust Ronan. Though she had never dreamed her trust would be put to such a test, she felt it now in her bones. All she had to do was get through these next few days. Ronan hadn't told her how or when he would come. She would have to leave that to her lord and master.

Smiling at Mordan, she took a sip of her tea. Still not entirely trusting the mind block, she gazed up innocently through her lashes, trying to read his expression. He smiled back, his face a handsome blank. Feeling more assured, she said, "This is all so sudden, Mordan. I'm sure you understand it's been something of a surprise for me."

"Yes, I can see where it must be," he nodded. "These things do happen, from time to time. Please don't take it as a reflection upon you, dear lady. I assure you that is not the case." As he spoke, he looked her brazenly up and down. Aria, still in her robe, clutched it more tightly around herself.

"You have three days left," he went on. "I am deeply honored to have been chosen as your partner for those remaining days. I hope to make the rest of your stay here as exciting as your first days have been."

He waved his arm, saying, "There are so many things yet to do. I want to take you sailing. To see your long hair, gleaming silver in the sunlight, your lovely form outlined against the sea! Truly, lady, you are poetry in motion."

He touched her arm now. She saw that his fingers, unlike Ronan's long tapered ones, were thick and blunt. Mordan was literally a Hercules of a man. The fact that he was so like a myth, like a romance novel jacket, somehow made this whole peculiar charade she was about to partake in easier to bear. He said, "That is not all I want. I want to strip you bare and taste the fruit of your sex. I want to hold you in my arms and claim you as you crave. I'll teach you the submission you are just barely beginning to recognize in yourself."

Oh! Pretty words. If only it were Ronan speaking them. At first, he had drawn the words directly from her own secret fantasies. But somehow together they had forged a magical bond of dominance and submission that suited Aria perfectly. She longed for him now. Again, as if he were speaking inside of her head, she heard his words, instructing her to accept whatever man they sent in his stead. To submit to that man as if he were Ronan himself. *You will be doing this for me. For us*, he had said.

Mordan's fingers grazed along her bare arm. Despite herself, she responded to it unintentionally, feeling a little thrill as he moved toward her collarbone and to the top of her breast.

"Aria," Mordan said, "stand up and take off this useless garment. Let me see you naked." As he spoke, he stood, pulling her up easily with one hand. Her instinct was to clutch at her robe more tightly — to resist this bold swashbuckler.

Mordan, noting her reticence, threw back his head and laughed, his chuckle deep and open. "Ah, the frightened little virgin, is it? I do so enjoy that particular human game. But no one will save you here, my lady. We're all alone. You belong to me, for whatever time we have left. I will leave you weak with satisfied pleasure. You are *my* captive slave girl for the duration. I am going to use you until you weep."

Aria gasped a little. She knew it was an act, and yet his words provoked something in her. This man's language was more flowery than Ronan's, almost old-fashioned, but his message was the same. He was acting off the same instruction, no doubt, as to her submissive sexual predilections. She found herself intrigued, despite a stab of guilt that centered around Ronan. And yet, she was only following orders, wasn't she? By submitting to Mordan, she would be submitting to Ronan.

A practical woman, she decided right then that she would try to enjoy the few days left, taking pleasure in the hedonistic offerings for which she had in fact paid quite dearly. *Waste not, want not*, she thought, grinning ruefully at the ancient proverb.

Aria felt trepidation, fearing Ronan would not be able to make good on his promise, however sincere his intentions. She would not betray him. She would wait, obeying his wishes and trust in him. Smiling now, she turned to Mordan and said, "Let the games begin."

Chapter Nine

She expected him to again command her to strip. She expected him to seduce her much as Ronan had, with kisses and sweet whispers, and his hard palm and maybe even the punishment cane.

She hadn't expected him to stand and lurch suddenly toward her. Sweeping her up in his arms, he bent down, covering her mouth with his, drawing out her kiss with a fierceness that brooked no resistance.

As he kissed her, he carried her to the bedroom—the bedroom that she and Ronan had so recently shared. He tossed her on the bed, his eyes boring into her as he pulled off his tight shirt and slipped out of his black leather pants.

Aria started to rise, pulling her robe, which had come open, around her nude form. "Don't move!" Mordan commanded, his voice like steel. She lay back, half expecting the force field to immobilize her, but she found she could move. For a moment, she considered slipping off the bed and running away, out the door, calling for Ronan, calling for 134256338.

But as she leaned away from him, Mordan was on top of her, his naked body heavily muscled, his chest matted with dark, curling hair. His cock was as large as the rest of him, and she felt it against her thigh as he leaned his full weight on her, pinning her down.

"You don't want me in your head and so now you are at my mercy, little one. As with any other human, who had captured you and now would have his way. I'm going to take you, Aria. I'm going to claim you in the ancient human ritual, using my body as a weapon to impale you, to fill you with my essence."

Aria struggled beneath the large man, a shriek of panic rising in her throat. With Ronan, she had known it was a game, albeit a lovely and sometimes dangerous one. But with Mordan it felt all too real.

She felt his cock, thick and hard against her thigh. Taking her wrists, he lifted her arms high above her head, holding them now in one beefy hand while he bent his head, seeking her nipples. Aria felt the wet flick of his tongue and then the sharp bite of his teeth. She gasped, struggling beneath him.

He licked and bit the second nipple and then kissed her throat, drawing his long tongue up her smooth skin, finding her lips and forcing them apart as he kissed her passionately.

Despite the fact that she was pinned and helpless beneath him, an unwilling captive, or perhaps partially because of it, Aria found herself deeply aroused, even as she continued to struggle, sincerely trying to get away.

"Stop!" she shouted, confused by her own feelings of loyalty toward Ronan and her instinctive submissive reaction to Mordan's dominance. "Get off."

Mordan laughed. "Oh, I know you humans. Especially you female humans. I know you have a habit of saying, 'No! No! No!' when in fact you mean, 'Yes! Yes! Yes!' So protest all you like, little girl, but it won't stop me. I'll have what's due me. You are mine to claim."

He stopped talking, focusing again on her nipples. Despite her fear and rising anger at his refusal to obey her,

Aria couldn't help the small moan of pleasure that escaped her lips as he skillfully teased to her nipples to taut erection.

Still holding her wrists in one hand, he moved his head down, his long hair tickling her body as he found her mons. He nestled his head between her legs, forcing them apart. His tongue licked along her labia, moving in slowly, slowly, toward her center. He held her still and took his time, licking and nibbling along her pussy, drawing out juices she couldn't control.

He teased her for many minutes, never quite reaching her center, the little clit that now poked its head eagerly from its hood. She shifted, trying to get his tongue to find the pleasure spot, and yet he would slip away, leaving her on fire, but frustrated.

At last, he relented, licking directly against the little nubbin, making her scream. Her mind shut down at last as her body demanding his attentions, which he happily gave.

She no longer even pretended to resist as her body flooded with pleasure, every nerve ending on fire with lust. When he finally raised his head, his red lips were wet, pulling back from white teeth as he laughed with triumph. His eyes narrowed on the woman now flushed, her eyes closed, her lips parted and slack.

Lifting himself over her, Mordan brought his hard, thick cock to her wet entrance and pressed in, entering her slowly, letting her adjust to his cock for a moment before thrusting his full length into her, drawing a moan that shifted to little staccato cries as he pummeled her sex. Their bodies were slick with sweat as he took her with sheer force. The pressure rose in a tumult inside of her as he moved in and out of her tight tunnel, still holding her pinned beneath his body.

She felt her own release mounting, being pulled from her almost against her will. For a moment, she felt she was with Ronan—this was *his* body holding her, claiming her. Only then was she finally able to let go and climax with this strange, strong man crying out his own pleasure atop her.

When at last he pulled away, Aria made a sound in her throat. Mordan couldn't tell if she was laughing or crying.

They did go sailing, and Aria thrilled to the warm seawater, watching the myriad of colorful sea creatures though the clear bottom of the boat. Aria always preferred planets with lots of water and life above ground. The dry planets generally were developed underground, with entire cultures existing beneath the surface, some of its inhabitants only dimly aware of "outside" and usually with no interest in it, other than as a means to travel to other planets.

This planet was so like New Earth she realized she could happily live here, in the little red-roofed house, with Ronan.

Stop! She silently admonished herself. It wasn't even his house, apparently, as Mordan now seemed to occupy it as comfortably as Ronan had, with full knowledge of where everything was kept.

Mordan was extraordinarily handsome. He was an excellent lover, though perhaps more predictable than Ronan. But then, he had the disadvantage of the mind block. She didn't feel a kindredness with Mordan, but he was exciting to be with. In fact, she suddenly realized Mordan was much like other lovers she had had, though

more outwardly dominant. He was, in a word, a good lay!
She laughed a little, not aware it was out loud.

Mordan, his eyes focused on the sails as he made some
minute adjustment said, "Are you all right? Tired
perhaps?"

Something in his tone recalled Ronan so vividly to her
that for a split second she fancied it was he there, a dark
silhouette against the setting sun. Her eyes felt hot and
stinging with unshed tears. "Yes," she said, her voice low.
"Perhaps a little tired."

Mordan skillfully turned the little boat, using the sails
and wind to change his direction and guide them easily
back to shore. He helped Aria from the boat. She was
wearing little black bikini bottoms, which contrasted
prettily with her now tanned skin and silvery curls. Her
high, firm breasts were tanned as well, the nipples a
pleasing chocolate brown.

As they alighted from the boat, Mordan took her hand
and then, without warning, pressed her down onto the
sand. "I must have you," he said, his voice urgent. Clearly,
this Erosian also savored his human form and its sexual
appetites, or else he was a consummate actor.

Whatever the case, he now forced Aria to her knees,
making her steady herself with her hands on the warm
sand as he crouched behind her. As if it were made of
paper, he tore her little bikini from her body and pulled his
trunks down only enough to release his already fully erect
cock. His hand probed her sex for a moment, roughly
taking its measure, deciding if she were wet enough to
accommodate his girth. He must have decided she was
because she felt the tip of his cock pressing hard against
her.

Her mind rebelled, pulling away from him. He hadn't asked, he hadn't prepared her! He was just having his way with her! And yet, her body responded, just as he surely knew it would—just as Ronan had known it would. Aria couldn't control whatever it was inside of her that thrilled to being "taken".

She loved the adventure of it. The delicious combination of fear and desire. The primal urge to submit to a strong man, to succumb to his demand for her body. Now she groaned as he filled her. His cock was too big and, at first, he hurt her as she tensed and strained against him.

But as he began to thrust and move inside of her, something eased and opened and she was receptive to his onslaught, pushing back against him like a bitch in heat. "Yes," she whispered urgently, not even aware that she was speaking.

Mordan took Aria under the hot Erosian sun, finally thrusting so hard against her they fell together, him still holding her hips, keeping his cock buried inside of her. Lying in the sand on their sides, he held her still as he took his pleasure, only letting her go at last when he'd satisfied himself.

As he finally pulled away, Aria stood on trembling legs and ran into the sea, washing the sand, sweat and semen from her body. She felt almost desperate to wash all traces of the man who was not Ronan from her body. She realized now what was different between the two men. Ronan understood the intrinsic romance of submission, while Mordan merely took what he wanted.

She dove into the waves headlong, remembering her first moments in the water with Ronan, and longing for him now so intensely she actually gave a little cry. But the sound was washed away in the crashing waves and when Mordan swam out to meet her, her face was unreadable. There was just a faint, almost bruised sadness about her mouth.

She turned away.

Chapter Ten

She'd played out the last days with Mordan, allowing him to "have his way" with her, though she found she could never give of herself completely. Now the last night had finally arrived.

And still Ronan hadn't come for her.

She felt increasingly on edge as desperation crept through her veins, sucking away the life in her heart. Was there any way, she had probed, pretending a lightness she did not feel, that she might see him one last time? Just to say goodbye?

"Aria," Mordan had responded, a flicker of irritation crossing his features, "there is no Ronan. There never really was a Ronan. Surely, you understand that. You certainly seemed to understand and accept it as you readily took me on in his stead. You humans are like that, capable of moving from one partner to the other with little thought of emotional connection. I admire that trait. It's so much simpler that way."

He grinned, perhaps thinking he was offering her a compliment. Aria only glared at him. She decided to ignore the remark, not wishing to engage in a debate about human versus Erosian behavior traits.

Of course, there was a Ronan! He was more real as a human than he had ever felt as an Erosian. So he had told her, and so she believed. This Mordan knew nothing about it. He might assume the guise of a human being, but he was cold at the core and without any intuitive understanding of her species.

"I can offer you money," she said, speaking what truly was a universal language. "More than you make in a year — in a lifetime. I only want to see him. I *must* see him." In the morning, she would have to leave. Her visa was up and her flight plan was booked. She had almost given up hope.

Ronan had said he would return to her. He swore it. And yet, the night was closing in fast, and soon she would be gone. "I have no use for your money, lady," Mordan replied. "We don't use currency here. At least not on a personal basis. Our needs are entirely provided for. I want for nothing. I appreciate the gesture. Nevertheless, even if you were able to 'buy' me with this bribe, I couldn't take you to Ronan."

His voice almost terse, Mordan added, "Ronan does not exist. That is not his name and he is not human. He adopted the form and the name to please you. Just as I have done. I hate to break the spell like this. It's most unprofessional, but I feel you give me no choice, Aria. The only way I know to convince you is to show you what I really am. What he really is."

He stood back then leaving Aria sitting on the couch in front of the crackling, cozy fire. Standing in the middle of the room, he seemed to change, right before her eyes. The dark thick hair that curled so handsomely over his strong neck seemed to melt away as did the eyebrows and stubble on his face. His head enlarged and his neck elongated. The leather vest and pants he sported fell from his body, and his genitals withered to a tiny flapping thing.

Aria watched in horrified fascination as Mordan morphed from human to Erosian. A long pale robe of shimmering gold now covered his sexless form and he nodded toward her. Only his voice remained the same as he said, "This is what I truly am. The rest was a fantasy created for your pleasure. A hologram, if you wish. A dream. This is the planet of dreams. Nothing is real. You knew that, and the contracts clearly stated it."

Aria stared speechless for several seconds. Then she leaped from the couch, pushing blindly past him, running into the bedroom, where she slammed the door behind her and leaned against it, sobbing bitterly.

Though the journey to the spaceport wasn't far, she found she had lost the desire to walk alone along this lovely stretch of beach. So much had happened in the brief week she'd spent on this strange planet. She was no longer the same buoyant, self-assured person she had been before love had snaked its way into her heart. Aria accepted the taxi lift to her ship. The little vehicle was preprogrammed and thus required no driver for which she was grateful. Mordan, mercifully, had respected her obvious need for privacy and left her alone that last night.

In the morning he had once again assumed his human, if bigger than life, form. He greeted her with a typically lavish breakfast of fresh fruits, baked breads and cakes, and hot tea. She had no appetite. She apologized, haltingly, for her behavior of the night before.

"I know it's not your fault, Mordan. I'm sure I'm not the first foolish human to fall in love with a dream. That's why you have all those contracts anyway, to render the spa harmless from idiots like me. This has been quite a week, at any rate. You did your gallant best to step in and be my 'lord and master'. And it was fun, as far as it went."

She looked so sad, her dark eyes turned toward the sea, her thoughts rendering her blind to its beauty. They parted at the door, exchanging a chaste kiss. It was hard to imagine this man had all but raped her on the beach, and made passionate and exhaustive love to her. She felt no more for him than for a casual acquaintance.

And yet, her heart was more than bruised. More than scratched. It was split at the seams. She felt broken inside, truly bereft. She had trusted Ronan so completely. He would come for her, before the week was out. Somehow, he would reappear and they would escape together. Her thoughts really hadn't gone much further than this. She only knew that he would come for her. And now the time was up, and Ronan was nowhere to be found.

Once the taxi door had sealed itself, she finally let the tears she had been holding back pour forth. She sobbed uncontrollably, sitting alone and huddled in the little taxi for several minutes after it had already arrived at her port.

Finally, she pressed the release and the door slid back. Slowly, as if her limbs were made of lead, she climbed the little stairs to her ship's door. They slid open as she placed her hand in the scanner so it could identify her as owner of the vessel.

She turned back for one last look at Eros. The vacation that was to have been a casual and much deserved break had turned out to be her undoing. She could just see the little house, with its cozy red roof, and beyond it the crashing, indifferent sea.

With a huge sigh, she turned back to her ship and went on board. It was something of a relief to be back in her own space, with her own things about her. She had had this ship specially crafted and fitted to her every need and whim.

It was programmed with the latest technology and she didn't need to know a thing about navigation or piloting the stars, though in fact she was quite handy at the controls. But now she took no joy as she looked over the flight plan that would take her away from Ronan, probably forever.

Even if she were to return to the spa next year for her one week "allotment", the odds were next to none that she would get Ronan again. Indeed, he had been "removed" from her, for having displayed too human traits, behaviors, and what she found most insidious, thoughts.

How horrible to live in a place where your thoughts were not only open to others, but read and censored by an authority that had control over your life! Aria was descended from the pioneers of space travel. If she had heard of the ancient sentiment from Old Earth, when separate nationalistic entities called countries had once existed, to "live free or die" she would have echoed the sentiment.

Yet, the Erosians seemed content with their lot. Well, they knew no differently. Except these spa workers, who had a taste of other cultures, albeit usually only a taste of their sexual mores and predilections.

Ronan had been different. He was apparently the exception that the authorities found unacceptable. And so he'd been reassigned, probably somewhere where they could monitor his mind, and keep him under better control. Poor Ronan! He would languish in that life. She knew it. He had been changed by his associations with humans. He had almost become one. How could he now go back to a passionless existence?

One without her. He had declared his heartfelt love. She refused to believe it was part of the game, part of the dream. It had been real! Ronan was real. He would live forever, if only in her heart and memory. She knew with certainty that if he could have come, he would have. He must have been thwarted in his plans. Perhaps even now he was doomed somewhere, shackled in an Erosian dungeon, helpless and alone. She gave a little cry at the thought. "Ronan," she whispered, "my poor love."

A series of sounds erupted from her control panel, indicating that she needed to enter necessary data regarding her coordinates and flight plan. Sighing heavily, she set her course, entering the necessary codes to activate the programs. She sat back, half expecting Ronan to come bursting into the ship. As permission to liftoff flickered across her screen, she finally lost all hope. The spacecraft lifted into the atmosphere and then broke free from it, casting her like a floating bottle in the sea, adrift from what she held dear down below.

She fell into a doze, as daydreams of Ronan eased a little of the ache in her heart. When she awoke, she realized she must still be dreaming because the sound of his little flute echoed in the chambers of the ship.

It was a tune she hadn't heard before. More merry and open than the other tunes he had played. She wanted to stay in this half-sleep, to keep the sound of the music in her head, even if it were only an echo of something lost forever.

Aria snapped fully awake, as the flute grew louder. She shook her head, saying aloud, "What? What is that?" Before she could even articulate what might be, her heart leapt up, soaring and doing loop de loops of sheer joy inside of her. Her mind said no, impossible, but her spirit only laughed.

He had kept his promise!

She stepped into the sleep chamber and there he sat, as big as life, as human as she. He was sitting cross-legged on her bed, shirtless, in his white linen pants. When she entered, he grinned, dropping the flute and standing, his arms open to her.

Aria gave a delighted squeal, hurling herself unceremoniously into his arms. They held each other tightly for several moments and then Aria began punching Ronan in the chest. "You bastard!" she said, her voice at once playful and angry. "How could you let me take off thinking I'd lost you? What a horrible thing to do!"

Gently Ronan grabbed her fists, bringing them to his lips, kissing each whitened knuckle. "It *was* horrible, and I died a thousands deaths, hearing your cries, my love. I had to do it. Because I knew they would have lifted your mind block upon your entry to your ship. That's standard protocol — you only leave with what you came with and a mind block affects the molecular structure of your brain. If you knew I was here, you'd have given us away. We would not have made our escape, my love."

As Aria absorbed this new information, she stared up at her lover with widening eyes. The full impact of what he had done finally hit her. He had come for her, as he had promised. "Ronan," she breathed, hardly daring to move, in case this was a dream, or a mirage, or a horrible joke her bruised psyche was playing on her.

"Aria," he answered. In those single words, they each conveyed the depths of their love. No more words were necessary as he took her in his arms. Slowly they rocked together as Aria's little ship hurtled into space.

Chapter Eleven

"How'd you get in here? I have all the latest security devices."

"Oh, that was fairly simple," Ronan said with a small wave of his hand. "I assumed your form, just for a moment, so I could access the palm scanner."

"Huh," Aria wasn't sure she liked that, but she was too curious about the rest of his story to dwell on it. "But how did you do it? How did you get away?" When Aria was finally able to tear herself out of his arms, they snuggled happily on the bed, his strong arm around her, she resting her cheek on his bare chest.

"And how," she said, sitting up suddenly on her elbow, "did you escape thought detection on board my ship? I thought they tracked your every move."

"I don't exist anymore. I disappeared."

"Disappeared?" Aria's confusion showed in her face.

"I'll explain it all, my love." He paused, kissing Aria's little upturned nose and then each of her eyelids. She kissed him back, grinning, but then said playfully, "Focus, man! Focus!"

"Well," he said, "When they took me away from you, I was reassigned to one of the central processing units. A computer lab really, where many of the personal records are kept on the population. Since I'd applied for the transfer before you came, they were less suspicious. I was told that I was removed from the last assignment because they feared I was being contaminated by the human elements in my brain.

"It seems I was far too susceptible to those elements. I was in fact 'becoming human' in some ways, which, and please take no offense, is repugnant to the Erosian way of thinking. I'm sure you're familiar with the ethnocentricity of many planets. It's a common conceit and one that I fear my people share. We assume we are the standard by which other cultures must be measured. We fail to take into account the beautiful and unique aspects of every culture.

"But they were right, you know. I *was* becoming too human. And the only part they missed, because it would never occur to them to look for it, is that I *liked* it! I find myself more at home in my human form than I ever did as an Erosian. But of course, this would be entirely unacceptable to the Elders. My brain would be scrubbed. If they were to understand how deep was my affinity for things human, how profound my love for you, they would have essentially 'erased' me. I had to disappear before this happened. I had to cease to be, in their eyes."

"So tell me! How did you do it? How did you 'disappear'?"

"Well, Erosians are quite docile by nature. We rarely disobey. It's only the younger ones upon whom the punishment cane is used, usually young male Erosians who haven't quite settled in to our calmer, proper ways.

"I was banking on this attitude, to convince them that I too had learned my lesson and was now happily ready to be reassigned to an administrative post, where I could peacefully spend the rest of my days programming computers and tracking minutiae until I tottered over dead at my station."

"Ronan!" The image seemed so absurd that Aria had to laugh.

He went on, "But in fact, I had a plan. It came to me as they were transporting me to the Elders for a lecture on overstepping my boundaries with you. They didn't disapprove of any of my actions—it was my feelings which offended.

"I apologized profusely, declaring that my human form had indeed begun to affect me, and I thanked them for rescuing me from that horrid fate of losing my Erosian essence. They seemed taken in and I was reassigned. I was given almost all of the pass codes necessary to infiltrate the systems."

"Wait, couldn't they just read your mind and know you were lying?"

"I *changed* my mind for them. Not in the way you're thinking of. I didn't change a decision—I actually *changed* the makeup of my mind. All Erosians can do it, but not all are as talented as I am at it." He grinned, looking somewhat rueful. "It's not a characteristic one is proud of, you know. At least, not openly. I suppose it's rather like a facility for lying in humans. Those who are very good at it don't generally advertise that fact.

"We Erosians learn to 'change' our mind, putting up a screen of sorts that blocks the true thoughts and emotions. Some people are so good at it that they forget which are their own true thoughts and feelings, and what is a smoke screen.

"I never got confused like that, but because I've always had this tendency toward strong emotion and, as a result, toward disobedience, I'd learned from an early age to cultivate the 'mind change', as we call it."

Aria was all ears, sitting up and hugging her knees, her face creased into such a smile that her cheeks actually ached, but she couldn't seem to stop grinning. "I accessed my file—134256338. I simply deleted all the records associated with that number. That part was easy. What was tough was getting access to the codes necessary to deactivate my brain chip.

"That's the way the authorities track us and monitor thought. But sometimes the chips are defective or malfunction and must be removed and replaced. Before they are removed, they are deactivated. Very few people have access to the codes, of course. That was one reason I wanted to be in central administration. I knew the codes were kept there.

"I befriended a programmer, and, I'm not proud to admit this, but I spied on him when he was logging into various confidential programs. I pretended to stand about chatting, but in reality, I was memorizing his keystrokes and biding my time.

"Well, it was simpler than I thought. As I've mentioned, such blatant disobedience is so rare that it becomes easier to accomplish when one is determined. I got into the confidential site, got the codes I needed, plugged them into 134256338 and voila, I ceased to be."

"And you did this for me?" Aria asked in a small voice.

"No, my love. I did it for me." She smiled uncertainly, and he went on, "I do love you, just as passionately as I swore before we were parted. I long to claim you now, truly as your lover and mate, if you will have me. But even if you will not or if things do not work out between us, I am here because it is the only place I can be.

"I no longer felt Erosian. I have become human in so many ways, crucial ways, that I knew I could never resign myself to that life again. I feel so alive now! So vital! So free! It wasn't even an option. I knew I had to find a way to keep this form. I shall stay as Ronan. I shall age as other humans do and die at the end of a natural human life span. I *need* this.

"But," he stopped and took Aria gently in his arms. He kissed her lightly on her soft lips and tears glistened in his eyes, still golden, the last vestige of what he once was. "But I *want* you."

"They were wrong, you know," Aria whispered, between kisses.

"About what?"

"Dreams do come true."

About the author

Claire Thompson has written numerous novels and short stories, all exploring aspects of Dominance & submission. Ms. Thompson's gentler novels seek not only to tell a story, but to come to grips with, and ultimately exalt in the true beauty and spirituality of a loving exchange of power. Her darker works press the envelope of what is erotic and what can be a sometimes dangerous slide into the world of sadomasochism. She writes about the timeless themes of sexuality and romance, with twists and curves to examine the 'darker' side of the human psyche. Ultimately Claire's work deals with the human condition, and our constant search for love and intensity of experience.

Claire welcomes mail from readers. You can write to her c/o Ellora's Cave Publishing at 1056 Home Ave. Akron, Oh. 44310-3502.

Also by Claire Thompson

Tristan's Woman

Beverly Havlir

Dedication

For Jim

The most wonderful man in the world

Thanks for the coffee in the morning and the backrubs at night.

Prologue
Pleasure Planet
2250 A.D.

"Fuck me harder. Stick your cocks in me. Please, harder."

Ava leaned her head against the square, one-way viewing glass, her fingers rubbing around and around her stiff clit. She was wet and aroused, small drops of moisture rolling down her thigh. Her breath came in quick pants, her fingers working in sync with the moans and whimpers of the woman inside Pleasure Room Three.

The Erosian pleasure worker disguised as a seven-foot-tall, green-skinned Barraccus grunted. "Fuck you hard, I will." He pushed the woman's dark limbs wider and reared back. With one rough thrust, he shoved both his cocks into her pussy and ass.

"Ahhh," Ava moaned softly. She dipped a finger, then two, deep in the wet folds of her pussy. Her moan coincided with the whimper from the woman splayed on top of the tangled sheets.

"Oh yessss. I want both of your cocks. Fuck me," she demanded.

As the Barraccus pulled out, Ava glimpsed the glistening heads of his two cocks. She whimpered in need. The top one was roughly ten inches in length, the shorter one at the bottom about nine and a half. She couldn't look away, and drew in a shaky breath. She could almost feel the other woman's pleasure as the Barraccus worked his cocks inside her pussy and ass.

"Oh God, oh God, oh God," the woman chanted mindlessly.

Her eyes glued to the places where the couple was joined, Ava pumped her fingers inside her pussy. Her breath quickened as she drove herself to the edge. Her hips pushed against her fingers, trapping the slim digits inside the slick folds. She parted her legs wider as she gripped the window ledge, seeking some surface to hang onto.

The Barraccus grabbed the woman's jiggling breasts in his hands and squeezed roughly. "Ohh," Ava whispered, feeling the caress on her own aching body.

The woman's eyes rolled to the back of her head. The brute bent low and pulled her nipple between his sharp teeth, sinking into her flesh. Ava's breasts tingled, feeling the sharp sting of his teeth as if he'd bit down on *her* nipples.

The Barraccus straightened and hefted the tiny woman in his arms. Her legs immediately clung to his hips, his cocks sliding home in her pussy and ass without missing a beat.

Ava bit her lip, watching the huge cock ream the woman's anus over and over again. The woman was in ecstasy, whimpering and begging for more. Ava felt her own climax approach, and pushed her fingers faster and harder in her pussy. The Barraccus grinned and bared his teeth—his gleaming golden eyes the only feature marking him as Erosian—as he fucked the woman harder.

"Two cocks of Barraccus. You like?" he asked. At the woman's nod, he thrust harder. "Fucking your ass and pussy same time, I like."

The rough words spiked Ava's arousal. With a great shudder, she came in a gushing orgasm. She flexed her inner muscles to draw out the delicious waves and massaged her clit in sensuous circles. Her orgasm went on and on, until her knees threatened to buckle and she had to grip the window for support.

Though hazy eyes, she glanced back at the woman who was still getting worked over by the Barraccus. It was clear she was in the throes of a powerful orgasm, her body quivering and jerking with pleasure. Her limbs had gone limp. Only her small fists clung weakly to the green-skinned giant in an effort to hold on. Pure satiation flicked across her dazed face, the look of a woman who'd been thoroughly fucked by her lover.

Envy knotted a tight fist in Ava's stomach and the pleasure she felt from her orgasm evaporated into thin air. It was quickly replaced by bitterness. She wanted—needed—a man to call her own. It didn't seem likely that she'll ever have that. The High Council had decreed that half-breeds were forbidden to serve clients at the Pleasure Palace.

Ava's lips curled in disgust. Anger, impotent and familiar, had her clenching her fists. By virtue of being born a half-breed, she'd also become a pariah. Erosians were a proud race. Except for pleasure workers, Erosians of pure blood were expected to mate with one of their own to maintain the purity of their heritage.

An ache started to throb somewhere in her heart. Her mother, a full-blooded Erosian, had broken that cardinal rule. Aleesia Sumerlin had fallen in love with an outsider. While she'd lived, she protected Ava and her twin brother Kell from the harsh realities of Erosian society. All that changed when she died. Her children bore the brunt of her mother's punishment. The High Council promptly took Kell, away and installed him in the compound for "training". Training for what, Ava didn't know. She still believed it was all part of the effort to keep her in line. Just the threat of never seeing her twin again made her do the High Council's bidding.

Her throat tightened. Loneliness was like a steel weight on her shoulders. She and Kell didn't belong here. Sure, they possessed the vivid, golden eyes that were the mark of all Erosians, but there the similarity ended. Unlike the rest, they weren't shape-shifters.

It was a very lonely existence. Even if she could get away, she would never leave her brother. And where would they go? *Nowhere*. Ava sighed, her shoulders slumping in dejection.

Once again, her eyes were drawn to the couple, who were stirring once more. A lustful smile tugged at the Barraccus' thick lips as he worked his cocks in the woman's slick orifices. They moved, thrusting in counterpoint to each other. In. Out. In. Out. But Ava derived no more enjoyment from the erotic scene in front of her. Instead, she ached with an inner pain that was a constant companion. The weight of loneliness bore down on her shoulders. How long had it been since she'd felt a real cock slide inside her pussy? *Too long*.

With a melancholy sigh, she straightened her clothing and made her way to the end of the corridor. She opened the door and stuck her head cautiously outside, peering down the deserted hallway before hurrying toward the platform to get ready for her performance.

Chapter One

Lush, thick brush provided cover for Tristan as he briefed Jed and Logan. "We've received a tip that there are at least two, possibly more, Karn'alians here at the resort. We are to retrieve them and get out." The two men nodded. "The Prime Ruler has issued a new directive. We cannot disrupt a kingdom's peace and sovereignty. We do not make ourselves known. In other words, we keep a low profile and find our targets before the Pagans do. Set weapons to stun only."

"Got it," Logan replied in agreement, shooting the younger man beside him a mocking look. "Hear that, Jed?"

Jed mumbled his agreement, flicking his weapon to stun setting. "How reliable is this tip, Tris?"

"So far, our source has come through for us every time. The only time things went wrong was on Exeter, when the Pagans got there before we did." Tristan's lips tightened at the memory. They'd lost twenty of their people when the Pagans beat them to the remote outpost. They had fought, even though they were outnumbered, but they had failed their mission. "It won't happen again."

Tristan glanced at the Pleasure Palace. The building was low and sprawling, spreading wide with various wings and sections. In front of the gilt-edged entry was a sculpture of two figures coupling. His eyebrows rose as the lifelike carvings switched from one explicit position to another every few minutes. The attention to detail was amazing. The female sculpture's pussy looked remarkably real, down to the clitoris that was briefly revealed as the couple changed positions. *Well, there's no mistaking what kind of place this is.*

The opaque glass doors opened automatically for clients to pass through. Two burly men stood guard on either side, primitive laser stunners holstered to their waists.

They're clear, Jed reported through their com-link. For security purposes, Cyborgs had the ability to communicate silently through microchips implanted in their ears. *I scanned them and they have no other weapons.*

Tristan nodded and signaled the two to follow him inside. One of the guards gave them a cursory glance as they entered the resort, but didn't stop their progress.

Inside, the temperature was noticeably cooler. The natural inlaid flooring was polished to a high shine, muting their footsteps. It was also darker, the lighting subdued and strategically placed. The air was fragrant with a soft, pleasing scent.

Logan sniffed experimentally. *My scanner indicates that the air coming from the vents above is mixed with some kind of relaxing agent. It's harmless.*

Indigenous plants provided a touch of nature amidst deep-cushioned seats available for lounging. Elegant and refined, one would hardly suspect it was a pleasure resort designed to cater to every sexual fantasy. Flat viewing screens flashed a welcome message and instructions in various languages. Humans mingled with different species in the foyer. It was easy to discern the clients from the resort workers, who wore short, silky tunics belted loosely at the waist.

Wow. Jed's surprise was clear over the com-link. *I had no idea Erosians were so beautiful.*

Tristan stifled a grin, his gaze following the voluptuous female Jed was currently admiring. Her breasts pushed against the soft fabric of the tunic, the thin material outlining the large mounds and leaving nothing to the imagination.

Logan rolled his eyes. *Down, boy. We're on a mission here.*

Jed threw Tristan a hopeful look. *Maybe we can find time for some R&R after we complete our mission?*

We'll see. For now we have to find out where our targets are.

Logan's snicker came loud and clear over the link. *Oh, to be young and perpetually horny.*

The younger man threw Logan a mild look. Jed's eyebrow rose. *I'm only a few years younger than you, remember?*

Let's concentrate on the mission at hand, Tristan instructed. *The informer didn't give us a specific location. We just have to do our own surveillance and keep scanning.* He strode to the bar area just off the main foyer.

Heads turned when they walked into the lounge of the Pleasure Palace. Though they dressed in clothing suited to blending in, there was no mistaking the hard physique under their dark cloaks. Their height alone placed them head and shoulders above others present. One glance at their faces, revealed by the cowls they pushed back, convinced observers that these men were not to be trifled with. The male patrons cast wary looks their way, fidgeting on their seats and surreptitiously groping for their weapons. The women cast covetous glances at them, sexual interest in their eyes.

So much for not attracting attention, Jed commented dryly.

It's your ugly face, Logan snickered. *They can't help but gawk at you.*

I have it on good authority that I'm handsome and irresistible, Jed shot back with a grin.

Who told you that? The women you have at every space station?

Jed grinned. *I'll be glad to throw one your way, Logan. Just let me know.*

Enough. Logan, scan for Karn'alian life force, Tristan ordered. His gaze swept the length of the room. With the different life forms that frequented the pleasure resort, they'd have to be careful and be on guard. A place like this didn't distinguish the good guys from the bad. The Pagans could be here as well.

It took only a moment to perform the scan before Logan spoke. *Negative. No sign of Karn'alian life in this room. Negative Pagan presence.*

With an imperceptible nod, Tristan strode past the long, curving, smoked glass bar that extended from one end of the room to the other. A full complement of workers busily dispensed colorful drinks in different-sized containers to the numerous servers who wandered around the lounge. He commandeered a table at the rear of the room, the position giving them an excellent vantage point.

Logan signaled a waitress. *Why don't we start by ordering a drink? Let's see what information we can get.*

A buxom server came over and gave them all a sultry smile. "What can I get for you?"

Tristan watched as Jed turned on the charm, the younger man's slow grin revealing gleaming white teeth, his light green eyes crinkling at the corners. His ability to charm the female species had proven invaluable on different occasions. "What are you offering?" Jed asked.

Logan's groan echoed in the com-link. The woman bent closer. Her breasts were in serious danger of popping out of her tight top. "Anything you like, stranger."

Jed's eyes took in the view with appropriate male appreciation. "Maybe a body shot would be suitable."

She threw her head back and laughed. "Why don't you come see me later? I get off in a couple of hours. How about I get you three a round of Neehaleese ale? It's the best in three galaxies. So smooth and so good, you'll never want to stop drinking it."

"That'll be fine," Logan nodded. When she left, he turned to Jed. "Can't you lay off the women even for a little while? We're here on a mission."

"She might prove useful—give us information," Jed countered. "We *are* on Pleasure Planet, the biggest playground in the galaxy."

"Jed's right," Tristan agreed. "We can't call attention to ourselves. We have to appear as if we're seeking pleasure ourselves."

The waitress brought their ale and deposited it on the table with a suggestive wink at Jed. With a naughty grin, he returned her wink and ogled her ass as she walked away.

Tristan surveyed the room. His senses were on high alert and he knew that his men were the same, despite their casual stance. Every mission was of the highest importance, whether they retrieved two Karn'alians or two hundred. Their race was in danger of extinction if they didn't increase their numbers. Millions of people had died during the Pagan occupation and the resulting Pagan War. An unknown number of Karn'alians had escaped to make a new life in other worlds. It was now up to the elite force of Cyborgs to find them and bring them back.

His lips curled with anger. The Pagans had enslaved his people, putting them to work in the iridium mines, then systematically slaughtering them when their usefulness ran out. The women had been raped and brutalized over and over again. And the children? Tristan seethed with a bitter fury. The Pagans had maimed the children to ensure they wouldn't be useful as soldiers someday. It had been a source of amusement for the Pagans to decide which body part of a Karn'alian child to amputate—an arm, a leg or a foot. He flexed the muscles in his right arm. A glance would show a heavily muscled arm, nothing out of the ordinary. But underneath the tanned skin was an intricate robotic arm, powered by a computer chip implanted at the base of his skull, able to perform a myriad of functions to aid him in battle.

Years ago, a handful of surviving Karn'alian scientists, with the help of leading doctors and experts from the planet Dakara, had created an army of Cyborgs from children who were maimed and rendered crippled— soldiers who were faster, smarter and stronger than the wretched Pagans. Tristan had been one of the Cyborg commanders who led the uprising and the subsequent defeat of the enemy. His bitterness at his fate, as well as his mother's death, had proved to be a strong motivator to fight. The Pagans were eventually pushed out of Karn'al and freedom was once again theirs.

He subdued the bitter anger that still festered within him and brought it under cold control. He wouldn't hesitate to kill a Pagan the moment he detected one. But first things first. He had to find his people and bring them home.

His gaze roamed the lounge. In stark contrast to the elegant simplicity of the foyer, the lounge was gaudy, bawdy and ostentatious. Garish artwork featuring females of all shapes and sizes in varying states of undress hung on the walls, clashing with the deep red wallpaper. The Pleasure Palace was a sprawling resort complex that attracted every kind of human and alien alike, all looking for sexual relief.

Logan indicated the buttons on top of the table. "Why don't we check what they offer here at Pleasure Palace? That's a good place to start searching."

Jed fiddled with the buttons and grinned. "What do you fancy, Captain? Pleasure Palace has the widest array of humanoids and alien species known to the galaxy. Even mechanical females and blow-up dolls, if you're into that stuff."

Tristan shook his head with a faint grimace. "No, thanks. I don't find it appealing to slip my cock into a fake pussy."

A three-dimensional image of a scantily dressed female rose between them, her melodious voice loud and clear as she recited a lengthy welcome message. "Why don't we summon the hostess to show us around? Maybe she'd be more help." Logan signaled a buxom female dressed in a sheer, diaphanous tunic.

The hostess glided over to their table, her golden gaze underlined by a subtle sexual interest. "Greetings." She acknowledged Tristan with an inclination of her head, her gaze lingering for a fraction of a second on Logan before sliding to Jed. "My name is Ampara."

Although she was attractive, Tristan felt no more than a kindling of interest. A check on his monitor showed that Logan, on the other hand, experienced a definite spike in his body temperature. As for Jed—well, Jed was interested in anything female.

"Would you care for a tour of what Pleasure Palace has to offer?" Ampara asked.

Logan was the first to stand up, not bothering to disguise his interest. "Lead the way. I'd be willing to follow you...anywhere."

Ampara's expression was lined with faint awe as they stood before her. Tristan was used to that kind of reaction from everyone they met. All of them were extraordinarily tall, their bodies packed with hard muscle. Although a couple of inches shorter than Tristan, Logan nevertheless looked just as menacing and dangerous. On the other hand, Jed's easy grin and good looks hid a skilled and ruthless warrior, a trait which had served him well numerous times in battle.

Ampara blinked before gracefully inclining her head. "Follow me, please." She led the way down the spacious hall. In this part of the resort, the plush carpeting muffled their footsteps. Sconces lit the way, their muted light casting shadows on the walls. Glass-walled rooms lined either side of the hallway, velvet drapes pulled back with gold tassels to enable them to look inside. A cacophony of ecstatic moans and pleasure-roughened groans filled the air.

With a graceful gesture, Ampara pointed to the first room on the left. "This is our vanilla package."

"Vanilla?" Jed asked curiously.

Tristan peered inside. The woman on the other side of the glass was lying flat on the edge of the bed, her head thrown back and her wet lips parted. A light flush covered her sweat-slicked skin and her perky breasts quivered. A man stood between her legs and fucked her vigorously.

Ampara gestured with her hand. "This package is for those who just want straight man-woman sex." She threw them an inquiring glance, her gaze containing more than a touch of curiosity. "I trust you're all looking for more than that?"

The eagerness with which Jed agreed was amusing. "Definitely. Vanilla sex is boring. I like my sex spicy and kinky."

"What about you, Ampara?" Logan suddenly asked, his voice carrying a hint of challenge.

A faint blush covered her creamy cheeks. "I like lots of things," was her brief answer before she moved on to the next glass lined room.

Be careful you don't crash and burn, Logan, Tristan's amused voice murmured over the com-link.

Ampara spoke again, shooting Logan a sharp glance. "This is the other vanilla package. As you can see, the room is divided into two. One is for man-on-man sex, the other for woman-on-woman sex."

With a dismissive glance at the man-on-man display, Tristan gazed with interest at the two women going at it on a red divan. One woman was on her knees, licking and lapping at the other's pussy with uninhibited enthusiasm.

Ampara raised one perfectly shaped eyebrow at Logan. "Find anything to your liking here?"

Logan chuckled. He stepped closer to her and rubbed his hard cock against her hip. "This is strictly for the ladies, Ampara. Would you care to find out?"

She turned red as the ruby pendant she wore around her neck, but didn't deign to answer. "This next package is the bondage room."

The room was decorated like an old-fashioned dungeon with chains attached to the walls at different heights and locations. A woman was manacled to a pair of chains that hung from the ceiling. Clamps were pinned to her swollen nipples. Behind her, a beefy man methodically whipped her plump ass with a flogger. At every stroke, the leather strands kissed her skin with a crisp *swat*, making her moan in excitement. An automatic vibrator attached to leather straps bound to her upper thighs moved in and out of her pussy. Wetness slid down her limbs, glistening damply under the lights.

Interesting. Tristan felt himself stir. There was something incredibly erotic about a bound and helpless woman, receptive to whatever pleasure her lover chose to give her.

He dragged his gaze away and looked over at Logan. His second officer was looking at Ampara instead of the display. He smothered a grin. Logan had that familiar gleam in his eye that meant Ampara would be in his bed sooner or later. Judging from the wary look in the woman's eyes, it would be much later if it was up to her.

Ignoring the suggestive light in Logan's brown eyes, the hostess wandered over to the next glass display. Inside, a woman was being worked by a green-skinned, muscle-bound, seven and a half foot alien. His two cocks slid rhythmically in and out of her sopping pussy and well-lubricated anus.

Jed was impressed. "You have a Barraccus?"

The alien with two cocks was rare in this galaxy. Hard to capture and hard to tame, the Barraccus could kill with one blow.

"Erosians are shape-shifters. That's not a real Barraccus, but this scenario has proven to be very popular with the women," Ampara replied.

"I'm sure," piped in Logan in a dry voice.

Tristan took in the erotic display behind the glass. "She seems to be enjoying it very much."

"Have you tried a Barraccus, Ampara?" Logan asked, watching her reaction with great interest.

She lifted her chin and stared Logan straight in the eye. "As a matter-of-fact, I have."

Deep, boisterous laughter rumbled from Jed's chest. He shifted behind Ampara and, with his hand, mimicked an aircraft crashing and burning. Logan gave him a baleful glare.

Tristan shook his head with an impatient sigh. This was not getting them anywhere. Somewhere in the pleasure resort were two of his people. He needed to find them before the Pagans did. With quick strides, he made his way to the end of the hallway and into another darkened lounge.

Tables and chairs surrounded a T-shaped platform set in the middle of the room. At the end of the stage were heavy drapes that were currently drawn closed, blocking out prying eyes. There a barely leashed feeling of anticipation in the air, the conversation hushed and excited.

Logan stepped up behind Tristan and reported over the com-link, *No sign of Karn'alian or Pagan life.*

I'm glad you could tear your attention away from Ampara for a moment, Tristan drawled over their secure communication line. Turning to Ampara, he asked, "What's going on here?"

As if on cue, the heavy beat of drums filled the air and gradually rose to a resounding crescendo. Every male in the lounge, human and alien, sat forward in eagerness, all eyes glued to the stage. Driven by an intense curiosity that he didn't question, Tristan edged closer to the platform. The music switched to a stirring, sensual rhythm. A lone spotlight focused on the center of the stage. The curtains twitched then slowly parted.

A smooth, shapely leg appeared. A strange fluttering sensation started somewhere in Tristan's chest. The hairs on the back of his neck stood on end. A voluptuous woman draped in thin veils swayed into view, dressed in sheer, loose pants and a top that barely contained her generous breasts. She undulated onto the stage, her smooth belly dipping and rippling with every sensuous movement.

Tristan's cock hardened instantly. His breath stuck somewhere between his lungs and his throat. His computer monitor flashed, indicating a drastic change in his body temperature. Tristan unable to take his eyes off her.

Long, golden-blonde hair fell down her back in glorious, tousled waves. Her lowered gaze hid the color of her eyes, the long lashes creating half-moon shadows on her cheeks. He was struck by the fullness of her rosebud lips and her small, perfect nose. The graceful arch of her neck invited a man's touch. As she swayed and turned, her breasts were pulled taut by her outstretched arms, their heavy weight straining the thin material of her top.

Blood rushed to his cock, lengthening it to its full size. His system showed a marked increase in his pulse rate as she executed a graceful turn, the veils falling around her in a filmy cloud. Tristan stood as close as he could to the stage, unable to take his eyes off her. He was mesmerized by the sexy sway of her hips. Every shake of her soft body drew his eyes to her womanly hips and to the plump curves of her buttocks. She was lushly formed, generously shaped, perfect for fucking.

Before the night was over, he was going to have her.

Without missing a beat, Ava's gaze was drawn again and again to the heavily muscled stranger who stood at the foot of the stage. His face was cast in shadows, making it difficult to discern what he looked like. One thing was for sure, he was as tall as a mountain. While everybody else remained seated at their table, he chose to stand. Nobody dared to make him sit down.

A frisson of awareness slithered down her spine. She could feel the heat of his eyes as she undulated around the platform. The detachment she normally felt at performing her sexy belly dance was nowhere to be found tonight. Her skin tingled with tight, prickling, hot and achy sensations.

The temperature rose several degrees. Beads of sweat formed on her forehead, despite the cool air that blasted from the cooling system. The rest of the room faded from her consciousness. The world narrowed to just the two of them. Every sway of her hips, every sexy swish was for him alone. Her dance became one of invitation. She didn't know what was happening—she only *felt* it with her quickened breathing. All she knew with any certainty was that she was performing for him alone. She drifted to where he stood right at the edge of the stage, pulled by an irresistible force.

Her gaze locked with his. Her nipples tingled, turning into stiff buds that pushed against the translucent material of her costume. Desire was a tight fist that knotted in her stomach, sudden and breathtaking.

I want you.

She read it in his dark eyes with startling clarity. Intense awareness snaked through her system, little fingers of heat drummed insistently on every inch of her flesh. Her dancing had taken on a sexual tempo. The heat in her eyes, though directed at him alone, was there for all to see. Her skin was hot, sensitized to the slightest breeze. Her blood pulsed in time with the heavy drums. The unmistakable proof of her arousal pooled damply between the folds of her pussy. May the Gods have mercy on her, she wanted him, too.

Tristan looked at her flushed cheeks and flared nostrils. His sensors picked up her arousal. Possessiveness swelled in him, the abruptness of the feeling taking him by surprise. The thick, coursing desire that rushed through his veins demanded fulfillment. She belonged to him.

Tension mounted in the room. All eyes were focused on her, mesmerized at the sexy dance she was performing. Tristan resented having to share her with the rapt audience. This show was for him alone. *She's mine.*

His eyes caressed her silken body. The loose trousers hung low on her hips, giving him tantalizing glimpses of her soft skin. His fists clenched at her sexy gyrations. She turned in a circle and slowly withdrew a veil draped across her chest and threw it to him. He stretched an arm out and easily caught it, sniffing it much like a lover would. Murmurs of envy rose among the other men, some clamoring loudly for another veil. The thick sexual arousal that gripped the two of them communicated itself to the other patrons present, hiking their temperatures as well.

By the Gods of Karn'al, Tristan, Jed muttered in the comlink, unable to hide the large, telltale bulge in his pants. *You're generating enough heat to light up the whole resort.*

Logan swallowed visibly. He was not unaffected himself. *Tris —*

I want her.

Logan laid a calming hand on Tristan's arm. *Be careful you don't attract the wrong kind of attention.*

Tristan cast a restless glance around the dim lounge. Every male within thirty feet was affected by the unmistakable invitation to sex she was offering with every wiggle of her hips, every bounce of her breasts. His highly sensitive sense of smell picked up the sweet scent of her arousal. Those tight nipples pushed insistently against the transparent fabric of her top, making his hands itch to palm them. *All because of me. All for me.* Another stronger feeling of possessiveness rose to his throat, making it more urgent that he let everybody know she was his. His cock, thick and insistent, demanded to be appeased. *Soon...*

Ava shivered at the intense fire that lit the eyes of the mysterious stranger, gasping at the electric touch of his gaze. She didn't know who he was and didn't care. The air became oppressive. She began to pant. Needles of desire raced up her skin. She felt feverish, hot and achy. She was filled with the overwhelming urge to take her clothes off and offer him her body and soul.

His dark eyes smoldered with an answering desire.

It was a sensual shock to her system. Her pussy creamed, spreading outward to dampen her labia and her upper thighs at an alarming rate. Her eyes widened at the tight, prickling fluttering that started deep within her. *By the Gods*. She was going to come by the power of his gaze alone.

The tingling in her belly gained in strength, gathering momentum. Her movement slowed, her slightest gyration sending waves of pleasure skittering through her susceptible pussy. Her clit throbbed. A moan worked its way past her throat as she came.

The music rose to a resounding crescendo, the heavy beat of the drum pulsing in time with the huge orgasm that slammed into her. Her lips fell open at the shock of ecstasy that swelled inside her. Her skin was slick with perspiration, her heart beat a rapid tattoo in her chest. All her motion stopped, halted by the tide of sharp sensations that pulsed inside her. Panting, trapped in his gaze, her body trembled from the force of her pleasure. *Oh God, oh God…*

Like a rag doll, she slid weakly to the floor. She was so weakened with pleasure that she couldn't move. With great effort, Ava raised her face to look at him.

He stood no more than a few feet from her. He watched her with a knowing smile, as if he knew exactly what she was feeling. It was one of those smug male smiles that said he knew he'd brought her pleasure and would do so again. Her spine stiffened at his arrogance. The brazen possessiveness evident in his eyes chased away the lingering pleasure that thrummed through her veins. Cursing her weak knees, she pulled herself up on unsteady legs. Just before she made it behind the curtains, she saw a familiar, burly man standing guard in the corner, his arms crossed, his eyes gleaming with speculation. Ava turned and ran.

Gold. Her eyes were the deep, shimmering gold of precious metal.

Tristan made an effort to control the heart thudding in his chest. He had felt every single glorious sensation that tore through her, shared every bit of pleasure with her. It drained and energized him at the same time.

He rubbed the soft material of the veil between his fingers. Her scent rose off the delicate silk, light and subtle, teasing his senses. Turning slightly, he speared Ampara with a sharp gaze and voiced the question plaguing his mind.

Ampara hesitated. "I'm afraid she's not available for one-on-one entertainment. She's a performer, that's all."

"Tell me her name." The command in his voice was unmistakable.

"Her name is Ava," came her tight-lipped reply.

"Ava," Tristan repeated under his breath.

"There are any number of women ready to cater to your every desire," Ampara offered. "Would you like to see them? You can have your pick of one, two, even three women."

It was like Ampara hadn't even spoken. He wasn't interested in any other but Ava.

The lights dimmed until there was near total darkness in the lounge. The audience began to leave, still exclaiming over the sensuous performance. Many vowed to return the next day to see her again. As Tristan listened, his jaw tightened with displeasure. If he had his way, she'd be performing that dance for him alone. "I want to meet her."

Ampara shook her head firmly. "I'm afraid that's not possible. Ava is not a pleasure worker. She's a performer." She smiled and softened her tone. "However, Pleasure Palace offers a wide array of choices for the discerning client. Please follow me." She strode toward the opposite hallway.

Tristan turned to Jed. With a big grin, Jed sidled up to him and drawled over the com-link, *Way ahead of you, Captain. I got a tracker on her.*

Tristan nodded, *Quick thinking, Jed.*

It's a small payback for all the times you saved my ass, Jed stated in a teasing voice.

Logan clapped the younger man on the back before he turned to Tristan. *Go. Jed and I will reconnoiter, see if we come up with something. We'll continually run a scan for Karn'alian and Pagan life force.*

*The mission—*Tristan began.

Go, Tris, Logan insisted. *Jed and I will do the legwork. Time enough for our mission tomorrow.* He grinned. *It's about time you had some pussy.*

It was true. He hadn't had a woman in a while. And this one aroused him with stunning swiftness. He couldn't wait to find her.

Jed and I will keep our hostess busy while you slip away, Logan reassured him, pulling Jed out into the hallway.

In the darkness of the lounge, it was easy for Tristan to sink deep in a secluded corner and check the coordinates on the tracker. The little, green blinking light was his target. She was swiftly moving north. Tristan vaulted onto the stage and through the curtain. He spied an exit door.

Looking behind him to make sure he wasn't followed, he eased out of the door into the inky blackness of the night and tracked her steadily through the dense forest. A different kind of urgency gripped him. He couldn't wait to see her again. This time, she wouldn't be the only one coming.

Chapter Two

Ava fled into the darkness, seized by the frantic need to get home right away. Only in her quarters did she feel completely safe. Her veils trailed on the soft, damp soil as her feet flew over the ground, taking her deeper into the woods. She knew the way like the back of her hand.

What had happened back there? She didn't know and couldn't explain. All she could remember for certain was the intensity with which she was drawn to the mysterious stranger, an irresistible kind of magnetism. Who was he? He didn't look like any visitor she'd ever seen before. The cloak he wore couldn't quite hide the sheer strength of his heavily muscled body. She shivered, though the night's temperature was warm.

The lust that glowed in his eyes had been there for all to see. He wanted her. She felt it deep inside her pussy where moisture still lingered. The possession in his eyes was unyielding. He meant to have her. So she did the only thing that she could do. She escaped to the safety of her cottage.

The automatic doors swished open with silent swiftness. She ran in and leaned against the wall, her heartbeat thundering in her ears. Only when the doors closed did she let out a sigh of relief. She sagged to the floor, putting her head between her knees, pulling in deep, measured breaths to calm the heart that was currently trying to jump out of her chest. There would be hell to pay if it were to reach Malek's ears that she had practically consorted with a client while performing. The burly snitch of a guard he assigned to watch over her nightly performances had been standing behind the stage curtain tonight, quietly observing, intimidating as always. She was expressly forbidden to have any contact, even minimal, with resort clientele. The punishment would be swift and harsh.

"Why did you run?"

With a shriek, she jumped up and found *him* standing right inside the door. Her eyes grew as round as saucers. He was even more imposing up close. Beneath his cloak, his trousers molded the thick muscles of his thighs and the light, almost translucent shirt clung to his chest. Her gaze slid up to his face. His dark, obsidian eyes were intimidating under the slash of his eyebrows. His nose was slightly crooked in the middle. His lips were firm, his jaw square. There was nothing soft about him. He looked dangerous, completely menacing. "H-how did you get in here?"

He shrugged, his sharp gaze raking over her in a way that was becoming familiar to her. It was a look of ownership, a stamp of possession. "It was easy enough."

Her spine stiffened, though she took one step back for good measure. "You have to get out of here," she hissed in a furious whisper. Her eyes darted to the walls with something akin to panic. She just knew that bastard Malek had installed closed circuit monitors in her quarters to watch her every move.

He followed her gaze. With a frown, he glanced at the walls. He held up a finger to silence her for a moment. Then he grinned. "Jamming signal initiated."

She frowned in confusion. "Jamming signal?" Then she shook her head. "No, no. That won't work. You have to get out of here."

He took one step toward her. "Whoever *they* are, they won't know I'm here," he stated with supreme confidence. "There's no need to be afraid."

Ava backed away, glancing with frustration as the distance between her and the door grew farther. "I don't know what you think you're doing. But if you think you can barge in here to—to—"

His eyebrow rose mockingly. "To what? To make you come again like you did back there?"

She flushed. "I don't know what you're talking about," she denied tightly. "You shouldn't have followed me. I want you to get out of here."

His eyes gleamed with heat. "Did you think after that cock-teasing performance you gave me that I wouldn't come after you?"

Her chin came up, fighting the lure of his deep voice. "I didn't perform just for you. I danced for everybody out there."

"Liar," he accused softly. "You danced just for me. Every move you made was designed to arouse me. Every sexy sway of your hips orchestrated to inflame me. It worked."

She shook her head in denial. "You're delusional."

"I assure you, I'm not." A half-grin played around his lips. "Do you need me to remind you of what I'm talking about?"

She warded him off with a hand. "Stay right there. I don't even know who you are."

"I'm the man who's going to fuck you tonight," he declared with supreme confidence. His gaze ran over her barely clothed form once more.

Ava almost melted from the heat of his gaze. She resisted the urge to bring her hands up to cover herself. She lifted her chin, the defiant gesture totally at odds with the tight peaks of her nipples pushing against her thin costume top. "You're so sure of that, are you?"

"As sure as the wetness that's spreading through your pussy right this moment," he returned with silken softness.

Her cheeks burned. *Damn him.* How the hell did he know that? Clenching her fists, she faced him with false bravado. "If you think I'm going to let you touch me, you're mistaken. One call and security will be swarming here in seconds."

He gave her a feral grin. "First, you have to actually reach the button. And I have no intention of letting you do that." He advanced toward her. Eyes widening, Ava took a step back, then another when he didn't stop. "Let's see how you feel in a few minutes, after I've gotten you in bed."

With a gasp of fear, Ava whirled around and ran to the safety of her bedroom. She'd taken no more than a couple of steps when his arms locked around her waist like steel bands and actually lifted her off the floor. She struggled without success, trying to pry his arms off her middle. Her blows didn't even faze him as he continued on into her bedroom. The breath rushed from her lungs as he dropped her on the bed.

She scrambled to her knees and tried to glare at him. She swallowed as, with a flick of his wrist, the cloak fell to his feet. He slowly, deliberately, began to unbutton his shirt. "You don't know what you're doing," she managed to say huskily. "You can't be found in here."

He grinned. "So I can stay if they don't find out?" He didn't stop until all the buttons were undone. "By the way, who are *they*? What are you so afraid of?" he added casually.

The sight of the taut muscles of his bare chest momentarily robbed her of thought. She blinked, trying ineffectively to clear her thoughts. "You don't understand," she breathed after a moment. "There will be repercussions if I'm discovered entertaining you."

His eyes narrowed. "Do you *entertain* all the time?"

"Of course not," she blurted out indignantly before she realized what she was saying. His pleased smile had her gritting her teeth. "Not that it's any of your business. Will you stop that?" she snapped when his fingers went to the button of his trousers.

He didn't even pause in what he was doing. He undid the button of his fly and lowered the zipper, as casual as you please, as if he did this all the time. She could only gape at him when he pushed the trousers down his hips and stepped out of them. He stood in front of her fully naked and fully aroused. The words she was about to say stuck in her throat. He was, quite simply, magnificent.

His shaft rose from a base of dark curls up to his navel. His cock was as thick as her wrist, capped with a broad, mushroom-shaped head. The sight was mesmerizing. The skin looked silky-soft in contrast to the steel-hard muscle it covered.

He took his cock in his fisted hand. There were tiny lines of strain around his lips. "Take your clothes off."

Ava gulped. "You...you..." She took a deep breath. "You have to leave," she finished huskily.

"I'm giving you five seconds to undress," he warned. "After that, *I* take it off."

She tore her gaze away from the stiff flesh that jutted proudly at her, silently tempting her to touch, to taste. "Listen, I don't know what happened back there. But we can't do this. I'm asking you to leave."

His eyes flashed. "Negative. I'm not leaving." He put a knee on the bed. Startled, Ava scrambled to the opposite side. Her gaze darted from him to the door, judging the distance. If she could only make it through the door, she could run outside and escape. But before she could even make another move, he was there beside her. Incredibly, she heard his low laugh before he hauled her against him and toppled back on the bed. Before she could even catch her breath, he rolled over and pulled her hands over her head. He threw a leg over her flailing limbs, effectively subduing her.

Panting, she glared at him. "I'm asking you to leave. Find somebody else to fuck tonight. You don't know the trouble I'll be in."

His face sobered. "I don't want to leave." He rubbed his stiff cock against her thigh. "I don't want somebody else. I want you." He bent his head and looked directly into her eyes. "Whatever trouble you think you'll get in because of me won't happen. I'll make sure of it." The last was added in a husky voice before he ripped her top in two.

She gasped. The sides fell away to expose her heavy, tingling breasts. He didn't even pause, just went straight to the waistband of her pants and pulled. The fragile material gave in an instant. Ignoring her hiss of outrage, he tossed the scraps of cloth aside and just feasted his eyes on her naked body.

His gaze was hot enough to melt an ice planet. Ava ceased to struggle. Her nipples puckered into tight, painful points. The rapt look on his face halted whatever words she was about to say. Nobody had ever looked at her in that hungry, *I-must-have-you-now* kind of way.

An answering longing rippled through her starved flesh. It was at that moment she conceded defeat. She was going to let this stranger fuck her. "I don't even know your name," she whispered.

"My name is Tristan," he murmured just before his lips swooped down to possess hers. With a muted groan, Ava responded with mindless abandon. Her lips opened under his, the sweep of his tongue across her lower lip the only warning she got before he delved into the dark cavern of her mouth. The hot flicks of his tongue were intoxicating, tasting faintly of ale and something else, something she couldn't quite name, but that was immediately addicting. She was drowning in his kiss, reveling in the urgent melding of their mouths. By the time he tore his lips from her protesting ones, she was breathing hard and greedy for more.

His eyes glittered like dark jewels. His tongue snaked out to lick her kiss-swollen lips. He smiled when she attempted to capture his mouth for another kiss. "We have all night," he assured her.

Ava pulled against his hand. "Release me."

The slow, sexy grin he gave her weakened her knees. "I rather like you in this position."

An unpleasant thought brought her up short. "You like your women tied up and restrained?" How many women did he have? Come to think of it, what did she really know about him? Who was he? Her stomach sank in dismay. What was she doing? He could be a killer wanted in five galaxies...and she could be his next victim.

He frowned. "I suppose I enjoy sex games, but—" He paused, then glared at her with something akin to affront. "I'm not a killer. Nor am I wanted in any galaxy."

Ava's eyes widened, bewildered. How did he know what she was thinking? *Was he a mind reader?*

"My com-plant is highly sensitive. It can detect thoughts and feelings, unless you have remarkable psy-control and you're able to block your mind waves."

Com-plant? Psy-control? What was he talking about?

"Com-plant is my computer implant," he explained with exaggerated patience. "There are some beings in the galaxy that have exceptional psy-control that can block probes into their thoughts and memories. Are you reassured now that I'm not a killer?"

She flushed. "I don't know anything about you other than your name."

In answer, he slid a thick finger inside her wet pussy. Ava gasped.

"Would your pussy be this wet if you were really afraid of me?" Tristan asked. Her reaction was all the answer he needed. He added another finger and began a slow, almost lazy, pumping motion. Her resistance dissolved in the face of such persuasion and her limbs fell open, giving him unrestricted access.

"That's right," he murmured in appreciation. "Open for me."

She should take offense at the supremely pleased, arrogant tone he'd adopted. But the swirling sensations he brought about made any such thoughts flee her mind. It felt so good. And damn him, he knew exactly what he was doing to her. Her temperature rose. She felt hot, very hot.

"You're registering a spike in your temperature," he announced, his tone lined with a mix of curiosity and arousal.

Ava bit back a moan.

He plunged his fingers in to the hilt. "The heat in your pussy is remarkable. I've never felt anything like that before." He stilled. "My com-plant tells me this is not the norm."

Ava looked at him in disbelief. "You're thinking about that *now*?"

Tristan had the grace to flush. "My apologies. I've never encountered a pussy such as yours. It's highly unusual. The more aroused you are, the hotter your pussy gets."

Her gaze slid away, slightly embarrassed. She felt like a freak specimen under observation. "It's a rare genetic quality I inherited from my mother. Not all Erosians have it." She wiggled and attempted to push him away, trying to close her legs. "Science class is over. Let me go."

He had the audacity to grin, easily holding her in place. "Ah, but we've only just begun." He resumed his movement, his fingers dipping in and out of her pussy. "I'm already anticipating the moment when my cock will be buried in this heat. I fear I might not be able to wait."

Ava glared at him with resentment. "I'm not here to amuse you."

He stuck his face close to hers. "The last thing I want from you is amusement. I want to fuck you until you can't walk. I want to bury my cock in the incredible heat of your pussy and just *rut* in you, until you set us on fire."

Her brain fogged over with his words. All thoughts of resistance fled. He withdrew his fingers from her pussy, the audible, slurping sound of her moist flesh clinging to his echoing in the silence of the room. Heat skittered along her spine as he brought his fingers to his mouth and sucked.

"So hot and delicious. You taste better than Kai-pana juice."

She shivered. Kai-pana was a fruit known to be an aphrodisiac. Its juice spiked one's sexual arousal and was said to enhance sexual performance. "I don't believe you. Kai-pana is very rare."

"Hmm, you're right," he agreed, bending low to skim his lips down her neck. His tongue snaked out to dip into the shell of her ear. "We found it in the farthest outpost of the Exeter quadrant. One sip and it would turn you into a raving creature, starved for sex and plagued with an almost unquenchable lust." He suddenly sucked on the skin at the base of her throat. "I'm thinking of giving you a drop. That'll give me just enough time to sink into your hot pussy over and over until I'm satisfied."

Heat pooled in her belly. His fingers skimmed down her raised arms to her side, seeking a breast and finding it. Squirming on the bed, she released the breath she'd been holding in a gasp. His big hand cupped and curved around the mound, holding her nipple between his fingers. He squeezed.

"Ohhh," she moaned, jerking against him. The pleasure was so sharp it bordered on pain.

He locked his jaw and gritted his teeth. "Tell me what you want."

He said she was hot, but the heat emanating from him was tremendous. With a small whimper she struggled and strained against his hold. Her blood turned molten and throbbed hotly under her skin. "Touch me. Touch me all over."

The soft stroke of his hand belied the lust swirling between them. The same feeling of helpless desire that had taken her over during her performance was once again weakening her limbs. The tight claw of want had a stranglehold on her. She wanted him with a totality that took her breath away. With a small moan, she shifted closer, as close as she possibly could.

Tristan bent low and nuzzled her neck, inhaling her scent. His tongue came out and licked her all over, driving her to arch her neck in invitation. He drew back and looked down at her. His lips were mere inches from hers. If she reached up, just a little bit, she would... When their lips touched, her eyelids fluttered shut and all thought flew from her mind.

He kissed her softly, running the tip of his tongue over her lower lip, before opening wide and taking possession of her mouth. It was a kiss that plundered without hesitation, a fierce and uncompromising taking.

Her breath escaped in a hiss of pleasure.

He was a master at long, languorous licks. But it wasn't enough. Tight frustration wrung a moan of protest from her, one he ignored. His big hand curved around the indentation of her waist, his fingers trailing sensuous patterns on her sensitized skin. Everywhere he touched left her with a simmering mark, trails of heat seeping under her skin.

"I need more of you," she sobbed urgently.

"And you will *have* more of me." He cupped her breast and rotated his palm on the stiff crest.

He was driving her crazy.

He raked her nipples with his teeth. The light, barely there touch did not even begin to satisfy her. She writhed on the bed. "Release me," she demanded in a whisper.

Tristan chuckled and shook his head. "Not yet." He prodded her nipple with the tip of his tongue, grinning at her moan. "So plump and large, perfect for my mouth." He pulled her flesh deep between his lips and sucked.

Ava gasped and closed her eyes weakly. The hard, rhythmic suction of his mouth drove the breath from her lungs. She arched against him. Her fists clenched. She was filled with the overwhelming need to touch him. Frustration fed the need she felt, and she whimpered in protest. Light fingers trailed down over the slight swell of her abdomen. Her skin tightened under his light touch. Her lips parted on a soundless moan, moist and needy.

His eyes were dark and hot as he placed her hands on his chest, finally releasing her wrists. A sigh of bliss escaped from her. She drew her palms over his taut, silken muscles. Ava gave in to her urges and rubbed her nipples against the incredible heat emanating from him. "Ohhh."

He slid down, curving a hand under her ass, shouldering her legs wide apart, opening her to his gaze. The look in his eyes made her shiver. This big strong warrior was looking down at her with such hunger and naked wanting. She swallowed. The intensity of this…thing happening between them was frightening. She bit her lip, smothering a moan.

Tristan reached up and brushed her lower lip. "Don't." He leaned down and took her in a kiss of complete possession. Her senses whirled. Hunger was a living, breathing thing inside her. She was ravenous for him.

Ava cupped her breast and offered it to him, the rose colored nipple stiff and aching. "Kiss me. Here."

He lowered his head and pulled the tip between his lips. At the contact, she groaned and pushed more of her flesh into his mouth. Sharp needle points of desire attacked her with every push and pull. Ava uttered a moan of frustration came from her lips at his light touch. She wanted him to suck her harder, deeper. She wanted him to draw her flesh deep into his mouth and *suck*.

"More. I need more."

Instead of complying, Tristan went lower and slid down over the slight swell of her abdomen. Hard hit by desire and anticipation, Ava writhed on the bed. She waited for his touch but it never came. Her eyes opened and found Tristan looking down at her, a muscle ticking at his jaw, fine lines of strain around his beautiful lips.

Tristan gazed down at her, lust surging in his bloodstream. Her cheeks were flushed and her eyes were soft and unfocused. "Look at me," he commanded, his voice strained.

Her damp hair stuck to her cheek as she tossed her head. "*Take* me."

"So be it," he declared in soft tones, his lips parting in a victorious smile. The soft skin of her abdomen beckoned. He slid down to his ultimate destination. Her musky scent assailed his senses, making his mouth water. He wanted to taste her on his lips and drive her over the edge of fulfillment.

The smooth expanse of her long legs drew his gaze as she twisted on the bed restlessly, opening wide and inviting his touch. He stilled, poised over the fragrant mound of her pussy. He couldn't wait to taste her. His flattened tongue snaked out and he gave her a long lick. "By the Gods, you taste incredible."

Her mound was smooth and hairless. His breath rushed out of his lungs, forcing him to inhale deeply. Eager to taste her, he pushed her legs wide apart, exposing all of her to his gaze. With his fingers, he pulled her dripping labia apart and concentrated on the little button of pleasure that was begging for his touch.

He bit at her, holding her steady when she bucked in his arms. Tristan slipped his tongue through her slit and plunged deep inside, massaging and tormenting the tender tissues of her channel. By the Gods of Karn'al, her pussy was indeed hot. A fierce tide of lust gripped him. He wanted nothing more than to bury his cock deep in her wet sheath. The feeling was primal. He wanted to establish possession. He wanted to make her his.

With a fierce frown of concentration, he slipped deeper, seeking more of her honeyed taste. He was enveloped in her private heat, the internal temperature of her pussy hotter than any other he'd known.

How the hell was that possible?

His cock brushed against the cool sheet and he almost groaned out loud, near bursting. Unable to bear it any longer, he reared up and covered her body with his. Fitting the head of his cock between the folds of her pussy, he pushed in with one great stroke.

Ava cried out.

Tristan didn't move, every muscle tight and straining. Dimly he noted his com-plant registering a large spike in the pleasure part of his brain. Beads of perspiration covered his face. He moved once, and had to close his eyes with the supreme sensation of being inside her pussy. He clenched his muscles, gripping her hips roughly as her heat surrounded his cock. He'd never felt anything like it. The small part of his brain still functioning told him he was hardly being gentle with her, but he couldn't help the need driving him. He withdrew and pushed back in with one smooth stroke, earning a strangled gasp from her. Right then, he knew she was with him every step of the way. Again and again, he stroked inside her, burying himself balls-deep in her receptive pussy. He heard an animal-like groan and realized it came from him. He pushed her thighs wider and rooted deeper. He needed to fuck her, needed to absorb as much of the rare heat of her tight channel as possible.

Clamping his hands on her upper thighs, he splayed his fingers and pulled open her labia. His cock ground against her clit every time he drew in and out. Clenching his teeth, his control snapped. Firmly holding down her writhing body, he fucked her, hard and fast, thrusting deep every time. The mewling noises she made barely registered in his mind. He wanted to last, but the feel of her pussy clinging tightly to his cock was his undoing. Her sob of fulfillment reached his ears. With a rough growl, he fucked her faster, gritting his teeth at the slide of his cock against her slick walls. Pleasure shot from the base of his spine. With one last mighty thrust, he came with a roar. He shook from the force of his orgasm and slumped over her. A slow grin pulled at his lips. If the way she gasped out his name over and over was any indication, he'd fucked her well and good.

Raising himself on his elbows, he pushed aside the hair that partially covered her face. Her eyes were drowsy, her cheeks pink. Tristan kissed the sweet curve of her jaw before he carefully withdrew from her and stood up. With a rueful grimace he looked down at his cock, expecting to see it singed and burned through. Although his cock was red, everything looked normal.

"A-are you all right?" she asked hesitantly.

His lips curved. *That's supposed to be my line.* "Just a little hot," he drawled. "Your pussy has an unusually high temperature."

A delectable flush spread over her cheeks and her eyes slid away. "I can't explain it. I don't know why I'm like that." She glanced back at him. "In your—er—experience, I gather that's not something you encounter often?"

He chuckled and shook his head. "I can honestly say I've never encountered a pussy as hot as yours."

"I'm sorry," she offered with downcast eyes. "I'm a freak."

He bent low to kiss her. "Nothing to be sorry about. And I don't think you're a freak. To be honest, it just about blew me away."

Her face lit up. "It did?"

"It felt incredible," he whispered against her lips. "I can't wait to feel it again."

"Oh." Her eyes turned sultry and inviting. "I'd like that, too."

With a smile, he lowered himself over her. It was true, he realized. He couldn't wait to feel the tight, *hot* clasp of her pussy again. Soon, he was lost in the allure of her body once more.

Chapter Three

Just before the yellow sun rose, Tristan was awakened by a call from his ship. He crept out of bed and walked out to the sitting room.

"*Speak,*" he commanded in low tones. He glanced back once, noting that Ava hadn't moved.

Logan came on the com-link. *I think you better come back here, Tris. It's urgent. We found something.*

I'll be right there. He severed the link and dressed quickly. He glanced down at Ava. She looked much younger in repose, her lips softly parted as she slept, the golden, curly strands of her hair spread out on the pillow. Something tugged at his heart, but he didn't stop to analyze his feelings. Just looking at her made him ache with a hunger that he'd never felt before.

Did she even know how beautiful she was? How generous and passionate and giving? As he stood memorizing her features, there was a sudden niggling thought in the back of his mind. She looked vaguely familiar, like he'd seen her somewhere before. He frowned, quickly searching his com-plant database. Nothing. If he had, surely he wouldn't have forgotten her?

He reached out a hand to touch her, only to stop halfway. He'd better not. He needed to get to his ship. *I'll be back, Ava.* Before he opened the door, he did a sweep of the outside. Satisfied that nobody was about, he stepped out and disappeared among the dense foliage.

At the outer edge of the forest, he teleported back to his ship. Seconds later, he was striding through the transport bay to the operations room.

"What did you find?" he asked without preamble.

Logan and Jed looked up from a bunch of imprints from the onboard computer. "There some strange readings here, Tris," Logan replied, pointing to the middle of the imprint.

Tristan looked at the readouts. "Karn'alian life force?"

Jed nodded. "Two. But they're different."

"What do you mean?" he asked the younger man.

"See here," Jed pointed out. "Karn'alian life force leaves a definite mark, a certain energy read that enables us to find them. These two are of varying levels."

Tristan frowned. "Which means?"

"They're not wholly Karn'alian," Logan supplied the answer.

"We think they might be descendants," Jed piped in. "But we're getting no other Karn'alian reading from the whole planet."

Peering closer at the imprint, Tristan looked at the coordinates of the reading. "They're far apart."

Logan's blunt finger rested on the paper. "This one is located in the middle of the city. Jed mapped it and we're fairly positive it's inside the High Council compound."

"And the other one?" Tristan asked.

Logan and Jed looked at each other before the younger man spoke up. "It's in the direction of the forest. If my coordinates are right, it's right where you were last night."

Tristan froze in shock. "*She's* Karn'alian?"

"I was hoping you'd be able to tell us," Logan replied quietly.

Tristan could feel himself reddening. He hadn't bothered to scan because he'd been too busy fucking her. He pulled in a deep breath, cursing himself for getting so easily distracted. "There's no other dwelling nearby. It's her." His lips tightened grimly. "Let's get a more comprehensive reading on the other spike. Then we'll head out to retrieve both of them." He turned away, surprised and pleased at the discovery. Ava was Karn'alian? Even better. Last night he'd made her his. This discovery sealed her fate. He couldn't wait to get his woman.

* * * * *

When morning came, Ava blinked the sleep from her eyes and rolled over. The space next to her was cold and empty, telling her that Tristan had left some time ago. She smiled dreamily. Oh, what a night it had been. She'd lost track of how many times she'd come. She stretched and smothered a yawn. There was a welcome soreness in different parts of her body.

With a sigh, she hugged a pillow close to her. It had been hours since he'd touched her, but her blood still sang. All night long he'd feasted on her pussy. She grinned. And other parts of her as well. He was a master when it came to giving pleasure. A little shiver ran through her. She could still feel the rasp of his tongue on the tender tissues of her pussy and her clit. He'd made her come so many times that she'd been weak and limp by the time he was done with her.

All the pleasure implements she'd used before were nothing compared to the real thing. Reality was *much* better than imagination. A living, breathing man with a fantastic cock beat a toy any day.

Would she see him again? Would he come back? With a dreamy smile on her face, she snuggled deeper under the blanket. Maybe he'd come back tonight. She hoped so. She'd love to spend another night with him.

But what if they were discovered? The thought drew her up short, stopping her daydreams. There would be hell to pay if the authorities found out. A long time ago, she'd lost her virginity to a boy who'd actually liked her before he found out that she was a half-breed. Since half-breeds weren't allowed sexual encounters, she'd been locked up in an isolation cell as punishment. She shuddered. She never wanted to go through that again.

Ava came back to reality with a rude thud. Nothing had changed. She was still a second-class citizen ostracized by a society obsessed with genetic purity.

A series of peremptory knocks on the door gave her a start. There was only one person she knew whose knock was as arrogant as that. *Malek.*

With her lips set in mulish lines, she pulled on a robe and opened the door. She deliberately blocked the doorway. "What can I do for you, Malek?"

The man standing outside her door was typically Erosian. Handsome and physically perfect, but hollow inside. He gave her a mocking smile. "Pleasant morning to you, too, Ava."

She hastily wiped all expression from her face. It wouldn't do to let this man have even a quick glimpse into her mind. Malek was a scheming, cunning, ambitious snake. As special advisor to the Erosian High Council, he held sway over some very important decisions and was privy to the goings-on inside the council chambers.

He smoothly slid inside, brushing against her so close she had no choice but to move back and let him in. She didn't miss the sweeping glance he gave the room.

Her knuckles turned white as she gripped the doorknob tightly. "Looking for something?"

Malek turned in a slow circle, his sharp eyes taking in the mussed sheets of the bed. "I had a report of a slight disturbance last night."

Ava schooled her features into a blank mask. "Disturbance?"

He stared at her for a moment before he nodded. "Yes. The guards I posted outside thought they heard a man's voice."

She tilted her head and met his gaze head-on. "They're mistaken. Why don't you check the vid-monitors you installed in here?"

Malek pursed his lips as he looked at her, ignoring her comment. "I want to remind you that you are not allowed to entertain men here. Nor are you allowed sexual assignations."

"How can I forget?" she snorted. "The guards you have following my every move remind me of it all the time."

His eyes turned dark. "You are a half-breed, Ava. A half-breed promised to the King of Neehaleese."

"You want me to whore for Eros."

Malek's nostrils flared. Ava glared at him in defiance. One's physical appearance had nothing whatsoever to do with the ugliness they harbored inside. Malek was proof of that.

"The Neehaleese ruler has taken a fancy to you. He's been waiting for a long time, Ava. Sooner or later, you're going to have to go to Neehalee and fulfill your part of the bargain."

"A bargain that I did not make," she snapped with cold fury.

His eyes flashed in anger. "May I remind you that the only way you can secure your brother's release is if you cooperate?"

She threw him a bitter look. "How can I forget? Every day I wake up, I remember that you hold my brother captive against his will."

Malek's smile was smug. "Yes. I'm glad you haven't forgotten that one small detail. If you care for your brother, you will not disobey the Council on this, Ava." He raised an eyebrow. "Unless you want him sent to the mining colonies?"

Ava's eyelids lowered, hiding the hate she felt for this man and everything he represented. The Council knew she would never let her beloved brother be sent to the awful mining colonies. "I know what my obligations are. You have no need to remind me," she declared in stiff tones.

His cold Erosian-gold eyes slid over her body. Lust flared in their depths, and a sliver of dread crawled down her spine. Ava drew the edges of her silk robe tighter together.

"There is another way."

Her skin tightened with revulsion at his words. She knew what was coming next—she could almost see the words forming in his mind.

"You're a beautiful woman, Ava. Quite stunning." Malek walked in a circle around her. Though she didn't turn, she felt the imprint of his gaze. She tried to suppress the shudder that tore through her.

Malek halted in front of her. "I could convince the Council to send another woman in your place."

Ava glared at him, anger welling up inside her.

He ran a fingertip down her arm. "I could give you a better life. Take you away from this little cabin in the middle of the forest."

"In exchange for what? Becoming your whore?" she retorted bitterly.

He shrugged. "You're willing to whore for an old King, why not me? I could secure the release of your brother and send him someplace else to live the rest of his life." His tone was persuasive, smooth. "Think about it. No more enduring the stigma of being a half-breed. If you were mine, nobody would dare say anything about you."

She sniffed disdainfully. "I'm not interested."

His nostrils flared in anger. "You would rather let that gnarled, old Neehaleese monster put his hands on you?" He advanced toward her. "He's pushing ninety. Rumor has it he needs extra stimulation to get aroused. He likes his cock sucked for hours, Ava, before he can achieve an erection." His lips parted in a malicious grin. "Would you rather do that? Or would you rather sleep in my bed and let me rut between your thighs?"

I'd rather die. She retreated until the small table behind her stopped her movement. "The Council has decreed that no full-blooded Erosian can mate with a half-breed. You can't break the law."

Malek's chest puffed out in an arrogant gesture. "You underestimate my power and influence over High Councilman Drago. A well-placed suggestion, a word of advice in his ear, and he'll be convinced he's doing the right thing in letting me have you."

Ava lifted her chin in defiance. "This alliance with the Neehaleese King is too important for Eros. The Council won't renege on the agreement."

"Do you think you're the first? Hardly. There have been three before you, Ava. Three women sent to the Neehaleese King to use and discard." His gaze was triumphant as he watched all the color drain from her face. "He's convinced he's still able to sire an heir, and when the women don't quickly become pregnant, he gets rid of them."

"You're lying," she whispered in horror.

"Believe what you like. But the Council turns a blind eye because they need Neehaleese aid too much to stir the pot." He shifted closer. "You're not the first and you won't be the last."

Ava swallowed the bile in her throat and forced her gaze to meet his head on. Showing him any kind of weakness would be fatal.

"You care about your brother, don't you?"

She didn't answer.

His lust-filled eyes roamed over her barely covered form, lingering on the soft thrust of her breasts against her silk robe. "You'd do well to remember that I could give Kell the protection he needs. It would be such a tragedy if he was to suffer an accident and perhaps...die."

She clenched her fists in anger. "You bastard!"

"Tsk, tsk. Name calling will get you nowhere." He touched her cheek. "I could make life very difficult for you and your brother."

Her eyes threw off sparks of amber fury before she averted her face. "If you think that threatening me will make me change my mind, you're mistaken. I'll find a way, Malek. I'll find a way to get my brother out of the prison you've put him into and get us off this planet."

"I do believe you just threatened to commit an act of sedition," he stated in a smug voice. "That will earn you some punishment. Guard!"

The door opened and a guard came in, holding his weapon in his hand. His glance flicked from Malek to Ava. "Yes, Sir?"

Malek strode to the door, pausing to talk to the burly man. "She threatened to escape. Take her to an isolation cell until further notice." He gave her a last glance. "If you know what's good for you, you'd do well to curry my favor. Maybe a few days' confinement will help you see things my way." His eyes slid lasciviously over her one last time before he walked away.

The guard grabbed her arm and snapped on magnetic handcuffs, tightening them brutally. Ava winced in pain and struggled wildly. "At least let me put on some clothes."

He shot her an evil grin. "Just following orders." He stared at her chest, exposed between the lapels of the robe that had gaped open in the struggle.

She pulled it closed, grimacing in pain from the handcuffs, and gave the guard a malevolent stare. "Touch me and they will kill you."

He laughed. "You're a feisty one, aren't you?" He pulled her roughly along, tossed her into the back of a hover cruiser and took her to a remote part of the forest. In a few moments, he stopped the vehicle and led her to the isolation cells buried underground. He took off the magnetic handcuffs and pushed her into the small chamber.

Ava landed with a small *whoof*, curling her legs protectively underneath her to soften her fall. Rubbing her reddened wrists, she looked up in time to see the smirk on the guard's face before the door slammed into place, plunging the cell into darkness.

Hot tears of impotent fury rolled down her face. Oh, how she despised that man! Malek was becoming more and more dangerous, far too aggressive, and this time he hadn't hesitated to dole out the punishment he knew she hated the most. She'd always been afraid of tight, enclosed spaces. She trembled, fear clutching at her insides. The isolation cell, buried eight feet from the surface, had no lights. A thin sliver of sunlight shone through the slats that allowed fresh air into the cramped, stuffy room. At night, it was the worst. It was so dark, Ava couldn't see her hand in front of her face. The walls felt like they were closing in on her.

She paced back and forth in the tiny space, wiping away her tears with determination. Malek would *not* win. She wouldn't allow him to win. One way or another, she would get her brother off this hateful planet. She had to think of a plan and act soon before it was too late. She needed to get Kell out of his confinement and secure passage to somewhere else, *anywhere* else, as long as it was away from here.

She would do anything to protect Kell. Her brother was her only family, and they had sworn to their mother to take care of each other. She wasn't about to stop now. *I'll get us off this planet, Kell. I promise.* How, she didn't know. But she had plenty of time to think, now that Malek had thrown her in the isolation cell. She had to come up with a plan. The sooner the better.

* * * * *

A three-dimensional image of the topography of Eros appeared before the three warriors. Jed pointed at a location in the middle of the image. "This is the High Council compound, comprised of ten buildings. Somewhere in here is the other Karn'alian reading."

"Security?" Tristan asked.

"Heavy," Logan replied. He punched some buttons and more images came up. "Security towers, one through five. Elevated, manned continuously. Only one entrance and exit and security clearance is needed." He looked at Tristan. "No clearance, no entry."

Tristan grunted. "We'll find another way."

"I'm already on it," Jed reported. "It'll take me a couple of hours. I've launched a subterraneous probe to see if we can dig under."

Logan shot Tristan a curious look. "So she didn't say anything that might have given you a clue to her identity?"

A dull flush crept up Tristan's cheeks. "Didn't have the chance to talk," he muttered.

Jed masked his laughter by pretending to cough. "I wouldn't waste my time talking either."

Logan stifled his own grin. "Good enough for me. At least we still have a tracker on our other quarry. We can find her easily enough."

Jed punched some buttons and frowned when nothing came up on the screen. "Huh," he mumbled.

Tristan's gaze was sharp. "What is it?"

"No reading on the tracking device. Let me try something else." Jed made some adjustments and tried to pull up the signal. "Nothing."

Tristan sought to calm the alien feeling of fear that gripped him. "Try again," he commanded in a calm tone. "She's still on the surface, correct?"

"We've monitored all departures, and I'm positive she isn't on any ship that left," Logan replied. "Jed, you're the best at this. Find her."

"I'm trying," Jed muttered. "Nothing's coming up. I'm not even reading the tracking device." He glanced at Tristan. "It's possible she's out of range, or surrounded by interference."

Tristan's went cold all over. *Where the hell was she?* Something was wrong, he just knew it. "We have to find her now," he decided abruptly. "I don't have a good feeling about this." He led them to the transport bay. Pressing a button, a panel slid open noiselessly to reveal a cache of weapons. "Be discreet. We don't want to alert authorities to our presence. Blend in. Find her and get out. Choose light weapons." He picked a menacing, five-inch curved Karn'alian knife and holstered it to his side.

"Do you want us to bring her here to the ship when we find her?" Logan asked, picking his own weapon of choice, a lethal pair of double-edged blades.

Tristan nodded. "Make sure she's unharmed. I want to know the second you find her."

"Sure thing, boss," Jed piped in. He chose a deadly sword and slipped it into its holster. Karn'alian Cyborgs were trained in the art of fighting with their hands, their minds and the use of their superior physical abilities. Even without weapons, they were a deadly force.

They teleported to an isolated spot on the outer edge of the city. Their arrival was automatically masked with a holo-imager, and only a slight distortion could be detected visually. At Tristan's signal, they set out in different directions. Jed and Logan headed to the heart of the city. He decided to go to the pleasure resort and start there.

Entering the ornate foyer once again, Tristan pulled the cowl of his cloak lower, hiding his face. He glanced left and right, deciding to walk into the lounge where Ava performed the night before. It was empty.

"There will be no show tonight."

Tristan turned to see Ampara, the hostess from last night, approach him on silent feet. He tensed. "Why not?"

She looked visibly upset. "The dancer, Ava, is—" she paused, "—indisposed at the moment."

"What the hell does indisposed mean?" he asked, his voice vibrating tightly. He stepped closer to her, a big, menacing, cloaked figure.

Ampara took a frightened step back. "I'm not at liberty to say."

Tristan laid a hand on her arm. "Do not be afraid. I'm not going to hurt you." He took a deep breath and sought to calm the voice in his head that was insisting something was very wrong. When he spoke, his tone was calm. "Tell me, where is she?"

She shook her head, clearly frightened. "I cannot. If anybody even suspects that I am talking of matters I'm not supposed to, I will be punished."

Tristan pulled her into a small, dark alcove off the hallway. "I promise you that nobody will know that you talked to me. Just tell me where she is. Is she…hurt?" It was hard to get the last word out. Just the thought of her lying somewhere, hurt and in pain, was too much to contemplate.

"Why do you care so much?"

The muscle in his jaw ticked. "Because she's mine. And I will do anything to protect her." His voice was clear, his words strong and sure. As soon as he said it, Tristan knew it to be true.

She looked at him, searching his features for honesty. To his surprise, Ampara burst into tears. "You've got to help her. She's locked in the isolation cell."

He stiffened. "Why?"

"I don't know why," she answered tearfully. "I was just notified moments ago that she would not be performing tonight, and that she's earned a stay at the isolation cell." She wiped away the tears pooling in her eyes and grabbed him. "You must find her, please. She hates the isolation cell. Ava, she's…she's afraid of small, enclosed spaces."

Anger began to grow inside him. "Where is it?"

"It's located deep in the forest. Please take care of her," she implored. She wiped the remnants of her tears with a trembling hand. "I have to go now. Make sure you leave undetected," she cautioned before she stepped out of the alcove and swiftly made her way down the hallway.

Tristan followed mere seconds later, walking purposefully out the front doors. Once he was far enough away from the resort, he contacted Jed and Logan through the com-link. *She's locked in an isolation chamber, deep in the forest. Meet me there.*

Without waiting for their answer, he set out on foot, heading toward the heavily wooded areas. Quietly, he stalked into the forest, every sense on the alert for any presence. Deeper into the woods he went, his rapid progress dictated by the overwhelming concern he felt for Ava. *She's afraid of the dark.* He refused to think of her alone and terrified. He needed to think, to stay calm and find her. *I'm coming for you.*

He came upon a clearing. Crouching behind a large boulder, Tristan observed a security building. A guard stood outside, armed with an electro-shocker. It was a device designed to deliver a shock that would quickly disable an opponent or prisoner. His fists clenched, and anger became a cold, hard ball inside him. If that guard had touched Ava with that electro-shocker, he was going to have to kill him.

Tristan circled around to the back of the building, and peered into a grimy window. Two guards inside, one outside. He observed the guard posted outside going down on his knees to check something. Tristan frowned. Were the isolation chambers underground? He waited until the guard outside took up his position once more. From there, it was easy. He crept up behind him stealthily. In a series of quick moves, he disabled and disarmed the hapless man. Dragging him to the rear of the building, Tristan tied him up with a restraining cord that was virtually unbreakable.

One down, two to go.

The best defense was a good offense. Surprise would be his best weapon. He strode into the security building, his steps deliberate. The guards snapped to attention and pointed their guns at him. Tristan smiled.

"Who the hell are you?"

"You have something of mine," he replied in an easy tone. "I've come to get it."

The tall, burly guard burst into laughter, one with a nasty edge to it. He looked at his partner, and they snickered. "Well, now. You and what army?"

Tristan didn't move a muscle. "No army. Just me." Before they could reply, Tristan leapt and disposed of their guns in a flurry of movement. Looking at their stupefied faces, he grinned as he tossed the guns out the door.

"Would it make it easier on both of you if you just turn your backs and pretend you didn't see me?" Tristan asked in a mocking voice. "I don't want to hurt you."

"We'd rather face a dozen Innundali soldiers," one snarled.

"Ah, but I'm so much more dangerous than an Innundali soldier," he shot back. The easy grin he gave them belied the intensity of his watchfulness, waiting for their next move. He didn't have to wait long. The two guards had no plan of attack, they just decided to charge him.

He eluded one easily, knocking him down with one well-placed blow. The other guard crept up behind him and landed a blow to Tristan's side. With a grunt, Tristan recovered and deflected a second blow. He pivoted and hit him so hard his massive body went through the window.

The second man crouched. He'd turned pale but his lips curled into a sneer. With a roar, he ran toward Tristan.

Tristan didn't move, merely balanced on the balls of his feet. In a move so fast his opponent had no time to react, Tristan flung him against the wall. He fell to a heap on the floor.

Leaving the unconscious guards on the floor, he ran outside. The isolation cells were buried underground, covered by thick, reinforced steel. He opened them one by one, his heart hammering when he didn't find Ava in any of them. He heaved open the last door and found Ava lying on the floor, curled up like a baby. Her eyes were tightly shut and her hands were wrapped around her middle.

He swallowed the fiery anger that threatened to choke him. His voice was gentle when he called to her. "Ava?"

Through tear-streaked eyes, she blinked up at him in disbelief. "Tristan?"

His jaw locked at the hope in her voice. Lying flat on the damp ground, he reached down and extended his arm. "You're going to have to jump and grab my hand," he ordered gruffly.

Ava didn't hesitate. She did as instructed and caught his offered hand on the second try. He pulled her up with a minimum of effort. As soon as she was clear of the cell, he hauled her into his arms.

"Are you hurt?"

She buried her face in his neck and held on tightly. "No."

His arms tightened around her. She still hadn't stopped shaking, and his com-plant detected her high pulse rate. She must have been terrified down there. Cold fury swelled inside him. He was going to kill those responsible and destroy all the isolation cells. A few plasma charges would do the trick. But first, he had to get her out of here.

"I'm going to take you somewhere safe," he whispered against her hair. "You're coming with me." When she didn't say anything, he drew back slightly and looked down at her. Her eyes were closed. He wanted nothing more than to wipe away the look of stark terror he'd seen in her eyes. But he needed to get her out of there first. He instructed the ship's computer to transport them up from the surface and fired off a quick message to Logan and Jed on their com-links. Then he picked her up, his heart constricting at the trusting way she held on tight and buried her face in his neck.

Once he got Ava calm and settled, he intended to find the other Karn'alian and get the hell away from here. Then maybe she could answer some questions. Like who she was and what she was doing on the pleasure planet.

Chapter Four

The ship door swished open silently and Tristan strode in. Ava gave him a soft smile from her perch on the edge of the bed. "Hello."

His eyes raked over her. "Feeling better?"

"Yes." She fingered the hem of the tunic she wore. It was huge, reaching to her knees, but it was as soft as butter and felt wonderful against her skin. In a self-conscious gesture, she smoothed her tousled hair, glad she'd freshened up before he came back.

Before he'd left her earlier, Tristan had pointed out where she could clean up. She'd peeled off her sweat-soaked robe and stepped into the micro-cleanser, the ship's version of a shower. She'd stared blankly at the empty cubicle, not knowing what to do. She'd jumped when a female voice announced cleansing would commence in ten seconds. Ava felt foolish as she'd closed her eyes, anticipating a rush of water. It was more of a spray mist combined with a warm gush of air and took no longer than a minute. But she felt refreshed and totally clean. On Eros, it was still the old-fashioned spigot with water. After her cleansing, she'd looked around Tristan's spartan quarters. There were no personal items around, no indication that it was even his.

"I want to thank you for getting me out of the isolation cell. I've never liked that place," she confessed with a little shudder. Though she was thankful she was no longer in there, she had other pressing things to worry about. She had no doubt that she'd have to face the consequences of her escape. By now, Malek would undoubtedly have been informed of what happened. That hateful man had leverage to use against her—her brother. She didn't want to endanger Kell's life. "I need you to take me back."

"No."

Ava swallowed and fought the immediate swell of panic inside her. Forcing herself to remain calm, she faced him squarely. "You don't understand. I need to go back there or things will be worse for me."

Tristan didn't move a muscle, yet he suddenly looked more dangerous in her eyes, more frightening. "Are you in any danger?"

Her eyes flew to his. The muscle in his jaw ticked and his lips were pulled into a grim line. "You can't get involved."

"I became involved when you took me deep inside your body last night," he drawled.

She flushed but shook her head stubbornly. She couldn't risk Kell's safety inside the High Council's compound. "I can't bring you into this. Please understand," she beseeched him. "I need to go back to the surface right now."

Tristan crossed his arms over his chest. "I want some answers, Ava."

Ava turned away, clenching her fists in frustration. "While I am grateful that you freed me from the isolation cell, my life is really none of your business." Malek would surely administer a more severe punishment once she got back. *Nobody* had ever escaped from an isolation cell. But she would gladly accept it to spare her brother any more suffering.

"I want to help you," Tristan said roughly. "I can't do that if you don't tell me the truth." His tone lowered, became persuasive. "Tell me what's going on."

She turned away, wringing her hands together. She knew next to nothing about this big, strong warrior. He'd taken her body, given her unbelievable pleasure, and for one night alleviated the loneliness of her life. Alternately rough and gentle, he'd made sure of her pleasure first before his. She *trusted* him, that's all she knew. Would he be willing to help her get her brother out of the compound and away from this planet? Hope began to slowly unfurl in her chest. The promise of a new start, a new life, beckoned. If Tristan could help Kell, why not tell him?

Ava took a deep breath. *I might as well start from the beginning.* "I'm a half-breed. Erosians are not known for their tolerance for mixed species. They're fanatic about the purity of the gene pool." She couldn't hide the deep resentment in her tone. "Half-breeds are ostracized, not allowed to mingle with regular society. Second-class citizens," she added bitterly.

"I know."

Her gaze flew to his. "You know?"

"You're half Karn'alian, Ava. One of my people," he revealed. "Our home planet is Karn'al. The Prime Ruler sent a platoon of Cyborgs out to scour the different galaxies for Karn'alians that escaped during the Pagan Wars."

Huh? "I don't know what you're talking about." She shook her head in confusion. "My mother was a native Erosian, but I never knew who my father was."

Tristan sighed. "A race called the Pagans once occupied many worlds and destroyed whole planets. They came to Karn'al and slaughtered and enslaved our people.

Many were able to escape. We fought a long war before we were successful in driving the Pagans out."

Ava couldn't believe what she was hearing. Aleesia Summerlin never mentioned anything about Karn'al to her children when she was alive. Her brow wrinkled, confused and shock by what Tristan was telling her.

"Our numbers were so depleted that our race is still in danger of extinction. The Pagans, or what's left of them, have vowed revenge on Karn'al. They are hunting down the Karn'alians who escaped their initial invasion and killing them."

"Your people are dying?"

His lips twisted. "Not of any disease, no. But we have virtually no women to bear children. And if the Pagans find our people before we do, they'll surely kill them."

Ava stood up and paced the room. This was all too much to take in. "You're a C-cyborg?" she croaked through dry lips.

His eyes were enigmatic. "When the Pagans came, they killed or imprisoned most of the able-bodied men of our world. The women were systematically raped and killed. The children were maimed in different ways to ensure they wouldn't grow up to fight against them."

Ava was aghast at the brutality he spoke of. "You were one of the children?"

Tristan nodded, lingering anger in his eyes. He raised his right arm. "My arm was cut off here—" He indicated his shoulder. "The same was done to others, some a foot, a limb, an eye. The Pagans made a sport of it, deciding which part to cut off a helpless child."

She swallowed, her heart constricting at the horror of what he'd had to suffer. "Oh, Tristan."

"An underground rebellion eventually formed. Scientists built a secret subterranean facility and spirited away all the children. The Pagans never bothered to look, assuming the children just died." His eyes took on a faraway look. "It took a long time before we all grew up and trained to be warriors. By the time we did, most of our people had died." He focused his intense dark eyes on her. "Karn'alians emit a unique energy reading. My men called me back to the ship this morning to inform me about you. You're part-Karn'alian, Ava. And I'm taking you back with me."

This was too much to take in, to try to understand. The only thing she could focus on now was that she and Kell finally had a way to get away from their horrible existence and start a brand-new life somewhere else. "I'm not leaving without Kell."

His eyes narrowed to angry, tiny slits. "Is he your lover?"

"He's my brother," Ava informed him with some exasperation, not noticing that he'd gone completely still. "He's being held in the High Council's compound to ensure my cooperation," she finished bitterly.

"For what?"

Her lashes lowered. "As a half-breed. I'm forbidden from being a pleasure worker. But the High Council has struck a deal with the Neehaleese King. I'm to be his wife."

The heat in his eyes as they roamed over her singed her. "I won't allow that," he declared with chilling softness.

She shivered, whether from the intensity of his gaze or the underlying violence in his tone, she didn't know. "It'll start a war."

He stepped closer to her, close enough to make her nipples tighten in anticipation. "We'll be gone from here before it gets to that." He stroked her cheek. "I'll get your brother out, Ava. That I promise you."

Ava rubbed her cheek against his palm. "And then what?"

"I take you back to Karn'al," Tristan muttered softly, bending to run his lips down to the shell of her ear. His arms went around her, trapping her in a hot, sexual cocoon.

She couldn't help but voice the question in her mind. "What then?"

He drew back, his face carved in hard, sensuous lines. "I'm not certain. Every time I look at you, I can't get beyond wanting to fuck you." She blushed at his frank words. "I keep seeing you in front of me, splayed wide open while my cock tunnels in and out of your hot, tight pussy." His big hands crept under her tunic and slowly pushed the soft material up.

A shaky breath rushed from her lips. Her pulse skittered madly as a tight firestorm of desire began to ignite in her. "I-I feel the same way."

He licked the corners of her lips. "You cast a spell on me last night when you performed your dance with the veils." In a flash of movement, he pulled the tunic over her head and tossed it behind him. "You're a sorceress."

Her lips parted, inviting him inside. "I'm not." She gasped at the first touch of his rough palms against her breasts. The slow, kneading motion he started drove the breath from her lungs. Her nipples puckered, pushing insistently against him.

Tristan skimmed his lips from the curve of her neck down to her shoulder.

"Tristan." In a move that surprised him as much as her, she slipped her tongue between his lips and kissed him.

There was no hesitation on his part. He responded in an instant and made the kiss his own. He drew her in skillfully, taking her deeper into the hot, damp cavern of his mouth. Wetness gathered in her pussy, spreading like fire, radiating out through her sensitized skin. Her breath came quicker, harsher. She wanted him so much.

The light teasing touch of his palms only whetted her appetite for more. Covering his hands with hers, she squeezed them over her flesh, harder, more forcefully. She glimpsed the half-smile on his lips, but she didn't care. She wanted more, needed more.

Taking his hand, she drew it down to her pussy, trying to push it into the sopping slit. But he resisted, instead exploring and teasing, swiping at her clit. She groaned in protest and pushed two of his fingers high up inside her. The low sound of satisfaction she made elicited a low laugh from him.

She tore her lips from his. "What have you done to me?" she gasped as he went deep. "Ahhh." The lust churning inside her was driving her beyond control, turning her into a crazed woman.

He sat down on the bed, positioning her on top of him. Ava straddled him, her legs on either side of his. She shamelessly ground down on his hand. Sharp needles of pleasure attacked her from all directions. Lifting her breast to his mouth, she offered herself to him.

Tristan took her nipple between his teeth and gently bit down. The shock of the pleasure-pain had her throwing back her head. He wrapped the long tresses of her hair around his free hand and tugged, arching her neck back. Then he feasted on her. There was no other way to describe the way he ate at her breasts, tugging, pulling and driving her out of her mind. The rough way he was treating her was exactly how she wanted it. She didn't want slow or gentle right now. She wanted fast and hard.

Plunging her hands into his short, dark hair, she pulled him closer. He opened wide, pulling most of her breast in his mouth. Ava shut her eyes tightly, a willing participant in the furious ride. She needed his cock in her. *Now.*

She fumbled with his trousers, moaning with more than a hint of desperation. When she finally eased his cock free from its confines, she made a delighted sound. The head was thick and red, a drop of clear liquid balancing at the slit. She licked her lips. She wanted him in her mouth so bad she was shaking with it.

Scrambling off his lap, she knelt between his legs. She pulled the pants free of him and tossed them aside. His cock was a hard stalk of flesh that jutted from a nest of dark curls. He was long and thick, and he made her mouth water with longing. With a small moan of hunger, she fitted her lips over the broad tip and took him deep with a slow slide of her wet mouth.

He groaned.

Ava was aware of nothing else except the hard piece of flesh she was savoring. It pleased her enormously to slide him deep in her mouth and lave him with her tongue. She wanted him, all of him.

Her eyes fluttered open and met his. Fine lines of strain etched his face, and he was looking at her with absolute concentration. Slashes of color appeared high on his sharp cheekbones. Wanting to drive him as crazy as this was driving her, she ran her lips sexily up and down his shaft, taking the time to lick the thick vein on the underside of his flesh.

His hips came off the bed. Gripping his thighs tightly, she slid down and licked the two spheres at the base of his cock. She pulled one in and sucked, lingering over her caresses. Making her way back up to the tip, she took him deep, as deep as she could, and held him there for a moment. The slurping sounds she made were delicious to her ears. Did he realize how hungry she was for him? She was going insane with wanting him. She wanted his essence, to take that part of him deep within her. She wanted him to come in her mouth. Maybe that would assuage this terrible hunger that was now overtaking her. She was so lost, so steeped in pleasure that she didn't notice the momentary stiffening of Tristan's body.

Tristan looked up as the door swished silently open. Logan and Jed stood on the threshold, wide-eyed and struck speechless by the erotic scene they'd discovered.

Logan opened his mouth to speak, but Tristan shook his head, quieting him. So his men stood as silent witnesses, watching the beautiful creature between his legs devouring his cock. They weren't unaffected. Their cocks had visibly swelled and were straining against their trousers.

Tristan cupped Ava's head and guided her movements, wordlessly urging her to go faster and take him deeper into her throat. She was a natural, her tongue skillful, her mouth a delightful cavern of temptation. The sight of his cock stretching her lips wide as she enjoyed herself was unbelievably erotic. His blood surged through his veins.

He pulled her up and positioned her on top of him. He took her lips in a hot kiss, lifting and squeezing the generous mounds of her breasts. He heard her whimper and felt her pussy brush against the tip of his cock. Her moan of frustration made him smile. Positioning her over him, he slid deep into her, sheathing himself to the hilt in one swift stroke.

"Ohhhh," she gasped.

He gritted his teeth as the heat in her pussy enveloped him once more, holding still until he got used to the unusually high temperature inside the slick walls. The combination of moisture and heat sent pleasure skittering up his spine, threatening to overload his senses. Grasping her hips, he guided her up and down. Soon, it was she who took up a fast rhythm, bouncing up and down his cock, stretching up until only the tip was left in her pussy before plunging deep again and again. By the Gods, she was a natural sensualist. His glance slid to his comrades. They had a clear view of his cock sliding inside Ava's pussy again and again. A thick surge of lust welled inside him at the admiration in their gazes for *his* woman.

Ava threw her head back and moaned.

"Look," he rasped.

She followed his gaze, twisting slightly to look over her shoulder and promptly froze. "Tristan?"

He didn't cease pumping his cock in and out of her wet pussy while he gauged her reaction. "They've been watching you, Ava," he whispered roughly. "Watching as you take your pleasure on my cock. First in your mouth, then in your pussy."

Her breathing was shaky. It was obvious she was torn between wanting to go on, and discomfort at discovering they were being watched. But he didn't stop the mind-blowing strokes in her pussy. He tunneled in and out, varying his speed and depth, making every effort to stop himself from spilling at the heat surrounding his cock. He watched her eyes glaze over with pleasure, watched her wrestle with her inhibitions. Gradually, she fell again under the spell of the desire surging through both of them, and her hips started moving once more.

"That's the way, Ava," he whispered as he tongued her nipple. "Show them how much you enjoy fucking me. They're mesmerized by your beauty, hypnotized by the sight of your pink pussy swallowing my cock over and over again." He sucked the delicate skin at her throat. "Does it excite you more knowing that they're watching you?" She whimpered. His fingers tightened on her hips. "Does it?" he repeated roughly. At her nod, he smiled with satisfaction. Lifting her in his arms, he shifted on the bed so that she was facing the door. "Look at them." He could see Logan and Jed reflected on the darkened window of the ship.

Her eyes flared with surprise, shadowed by temptation.

"Look at them and let them see you. It's all right," he soothed when she made a small protest. "It's all right to let them see. If they could feel the heat from your pussy, they'd never last. You're so hot, you feel so good."

Ava tore her gaze away from him to look at the two men watching them fuck. A tight fist of desire curled inside Tristan. She had that lost look of somebody so immersed in pleasure, so lost in the moment, she didn't care who saw her. He slipped a finger between her lips, stifling a groan when she immediately started sucking. He heard a choked moan, and didn't know whether it came from Logan or Jed.

"Play with your nipples," he commanded, never ceasing in fucking her willing pussy. Her small hands cupped her heavy breasts, her fingers pinching and pulling at the stiff tips. "Tell me what you're feeling, Ava. Tell me what you want." He kept his gaze on the images reflected on the window, at the graceful line of Ava's back and beyond that, his men's rapt gazes as they watched her undulate on his lap.

"Fuck me, Tristan. Fuck me hard and deep," she sobbed brokenly.

At her impassioned plea, Logan began to rub his stiff cock. Jed wasn't faring any better, his fists clenching, affected by the sight of the woman bouncing hungrily on Tristan's lap.

Tristan gritted his teeth as the pleasure swelled inside him. He was going to come soon, he could feel it. The heat was tremendous. Cupping the plump cheeks of her ass, he lifted her higher and plunged deeper, the sweet sound of her moan reaching his ears.

He lost awareness of the two watching. Now he was intent on pushing them both over the edge. Ava was making sexy, tortured mewling noises above him. It spurred him on. The ride was furious, rough and fast. He gritted his teeth, feeling the beginnings of her orgasm. Her pussy tightened and contracted on his cock and he almost lost it. He didn't let go of his control until he heard her scream and felt her shudder violently. Only then did he give one mighty thrust and shoot off deep inside her pussy.

Afterwards, Ava was slumped over him, her face shiny with sweat. He hugged her tight, his flesh still pulsing deep inside her. He drew back, feeling her stiffen. "What's wrong?"

Her cheeks were a deep red. "Those two men…" she trailed off and took a deep breath. "They were watching us."

Tristan gently pushed her hair back. "Does it bother you?" She bowed her head. He tipped her chin up. "They enjoyed it as much as we did, Ava. You shouldn't be ashamed. You were so beautiful, lost in the throes of pleasure. I was proud to have them witness that."

She buried her face in his neck. "I'll never be able to face them, whoever they are."

He chuckled, feeling relaxed and replete. "They're my comrades, my second- and third-in-command. We've been together for a long time. They're like my brothers." He paused. "I like it that they watched me fucking you, giving you pleasure."

She mumbled something he didn't understand.

"It was exciting, was it not?" he asked softly. "It excited you, knowing that they were so affected, so aroused."

Her lashes lowered, hiding her eyes from him.

He smiled. "You aroused them, Ava. They watched you play with your breasts and they almost couldn't help themselves. It's natural to revel in somebody's admiration. Don't be embarrassed."

She released a sigh, the sound a mixture of acceptance and resignation. "It's all your fault. You've turned me into a wanton hussy."

Possessiveness welled inside him and he pulled her close. "We'll get your brother out of the High Council's compound. Then I'm taking you back to Karn'al where you belong."

Chapter Five

Ava walked into the operations room of the ship, her fingers intertwined with Tristan's. Hot color flooded her cheeks at the sight of the two men standing in the middle of the room.

She made herself look them in the eye as Tristan performed the introductions, refusing to look away. Both men were tall and built, with muscles that rippled with obvious strength. Logan was older, his face harsher, but there was a sensuality inherent in the firm slash of his lips. Jed was younger and very good-looking, charming and confident, judging from the sensual light that lurked in his deep green eyes.

Sexual tension thickened the air, but it was gone quickly. The men were once again looking at her with polite regard. She flushed, confused by the tightening of her nipples under the tunic. A low, insistent throbbing started in her pussy.

Ava didn't see the grin that Tristan quickly stifled. He turned to his men. "Her brother is the other energy spike we've been picking up." Logan and Jed nodded. "He's being held inside the High Council compound."

He walked toward a three-sided, complicated-looking console. It was full of buttons that blinked incessantly. Tristan pressed one in front of him. Ava's eyes widened as a realistic-looking, three-dimensional map of Eros came up between the three men.

Tristan examined the map. "We need to get in and out without alerting the guards."

Logan grunted. "I'm in the mood for a fight. Why don't we take the whole lot of them on?"

Jed's lips curved. "Sounds like fun to me."

Tristan shook his head firmly. "Ordinarily, I'd be all for it, too. Except we got word that a Pagan cruiser has been spotted heading here."

Logan grinned with relish. "Even better."

"We can't wait for them to get here. We get Ava's brother and we get out." Tristan cocked an eyebrow at Jed. "Anything from the subterranean probe?"

"Negative," Jed replied. "I found no other way in. Like I said, one way in, one way out."

Ava watched this exchange with interest. Tristan was every inch the commander, his bearing tall and straight, inspiring confidence with his strength. Jed and Logan were no less intimidating, their casual confidence a clear indication of their skills in combat.

Logan gestured to the towers. "Guards are changed every four hours. One guard stays inside the tower, one patrols the walkway. It takes five minutes to walk from one end to the other."

Tristan placed his palms on the console and leaned in. "Weapons?"

"Very primitive," Jed replied. "They have a variety of them, from laser to old-fashioned, bullet-equipped guns."

Tristan considered the map for a moment. "We go in here." He pointed to the corner tower before turning to Jed. "Can we lock on to the energy signal?"

"It fades in and out. There's too much interference in the compound," Jed replied. "They're using some sort of low-level signal to jam electronic devices."

"So we can't just teleport out of there after we find him?" Logan asked.

"Negative." Jed pushed some more buttons on the console. "We're going to have to do this the old-fashioned way. We have to retrieve the target and get some distance away from the compound to teleport back here."

Tristan grunted. "Fine. We go in, get our target and get out. We have to make it to a safe teleporting distance with a minimum of fuss. We don't want the Pagans alerted of our activities."

"That's too bad," Jed drawled in mock regret. "I'm just itchin' for a fight."

Logan muttered his agreement, but they didn't oppose Tristan's plan. Ava spoke up. "I want to go with you."

"No," Tristan answered without even looking at her.

She bristled at being dismissed so easily. "He's my brother." She lifted her chin. "You don't have the right to stop me from going."

Logan and Jed looked on with foolish grins on their faces, waiting for Tristan's answer. He shot them a quelling glare before facing her, his stance one of exaggerated patience. "It may get messy down there. My men and I need to focus on retrieving the target, not have to worry about your ass."

Her eyes narrowed. "My ass will be perfectly fine. I'm not a dimwit. I know enough to stay out of danger." She felt a moment of trepidation as his eyes hardened but she refused to back down. She wanted to go, dammit.

"You will do as you're told and stay here on the ship, awaiting our return." His tone and countenance didn't change, but just the same Ava swallowed the lump that suddenly lodged in her throat.

She gritted her teeth in frustration. "Kell does not know what's going on. If I'm there, he'll come without resistance."

Jed's lips curved in amusement. "I don't think he'll be in any position to refuse us."

Ava shot him an irritated glance. Men. They were all the same. They stuck with each other, like some sort of primal tribal thing. She turned to Tristan. "I'm asking you again. Let me go with you. I haven't seen my brother in a long time. I won't be any trouble, I assure you. Kell will understand better and come willingly if I'm there," she reiterated.

Tristan's dark, inscrutable gaze stayed on her for long moments before he sighed. "Fine. But you will do exactly what we tell you. If you lag behind or we run into trouble because of you, I won't hesitate to take you back here in a second, do you understand me?"

Pleased at her small victory, she nodded eagerly. "Thank you."

"We'll be ready to go as soon as it turns dark," Tristan informed them. "Ava, you'll find some clothes in my quarters." His eyes traveled down her bare legs. "Much as I like the sight of you with only that tunic on, you'll need more clothing than that."

Her cheeks flaming, Ava shot him a glare that promised reprisals later, before she walked out with her head held high. As soon as the door swished closed behind her, Logan chuckled.

"With all due respect, Tris, I think having some pussy has made you soft."

Jed grinned, nodding in agreement. "I agree."

A smile played around Tristan's lips. "It's hard to say no to her. She's something else."

"We know. We were there, remember?" Logan murmured.

"I take it that you haven't told her about the Ritual of Acceptance?" Jed asked carefully.

Tristan grimaced. "Not yet. It's too early to tell if she's *it* for me."

Logan's eyebrow rose. "Will you be able to let her go once we take her back to Karn'al?"

He sighed. "I don't know. I haven't exactly given it any thought."

"Somebody will claim her, if you don't," Logan reminded him. "The policy to procreate is of the utmost importance. She'll be placed on the list for immediate claiming."

A sigh blew from Tristan's grim lips. Procreation was high up on the Prime Ruler's list of goals. Due to the near extinction of their race, unclaimed Karn'alian women were required to submit to the harvesting of their eggs to match with male donors so that scientists could proceed with procreation experiments. The thousands of Karn'alians expected to be brought back home were needed to expand the gene pool. But the Prime Ruler had made it clear that artificial reproduction was to be the last resort. He wanted breeding done the natural way. As a result, Karn'alian men were required to claim women as their mates as soon as possible. As soon as Ava arrived on Karn'al, she would be placed on the claiming list. That gave him pause. The thought of some other man laying a hand on Ava brought an odd sense of tension in him.

"Logan's right," Jed spoke up. "A little pussy on the side is fine, but when we take her back, you know she'll be claimed, unless *you* claim her as yours first."

Tristan ran his hands through his hair. "I realize that. The thought of somebody else touching her..." he trailed off, the unspoken words hanging over them.

"If you do claim her," Logan began in a soft tone, "you have to tell her of the ritual. You have to make her understand its necessity. From what Jed and I saw earlier, I don't think she'll be opposed to it."

Ambivalence gnawed at Tristan. The Ritual of Acceptance existed among the Cyborg warriors. One had to share his claimed woman *for one time only* with one of his comrades. If he claimed Ava as his, he'd have to share her with either Logan or Jed. If he died in battle, the ritual would mean that Logan or Jed would take his place, ensuring the continuity of the Karn'alian line and assuming responsibility for Ava's well-being. How would Ava react to that? Would she be open to the idea? He recalled her reaction when she'd spotted Logan and Jed watching them from the doorway. She'd been uncomfortable initially, but he knew she found it exciting that they were being watched while they fucked. Maybe with the right preparation and stimulation, she'd be open to the idea of letting another man join them in bed *once* to complete the ritual.

He clamped his jaw. Just one time, that's all he needed to do to fulfill the damned ritual. Any more than that and he didn't think he could do it, certainly not on a regular basis. "I'll think about it," he said when he finally spoke. "We leave at dusk. Get ready."

He turned and left, honest enough with himself to admit that there was a measure of excitement at the thought of the pleasure he and another man could give Ava.

Chapter Six

Tristan followed Jed down the narrow hallway. The tracker Jed held in his hand was locked on the energy output from Ava's brother. His restless, alert eyes surveyed the path up ahead. He didn't like the feel of things. It had been way too easy. They were able to get in with hardly any problem at all. There weren't any guards posted anywhere in the building.

Something's not right, he warned Logan and Jed over the com-link. *It's too easy.*

Almost like they're expecting us, Logan remarked.

I don't have a good feeling about this either, Jed put in. *We're almost there. Hey, Logan*, he added. *Maybe we'll get the fight we've been hankering for.*

Bring it on, Logan countered with more than a hint of relish in his voice.

Be alert for anything, Tristan instructed. *We get him and get out.*

Aww, Tris, Logan drawled mockingly. *Where's the fun in that?*

We'll have fun later. Right now, he ordered firmly, *we get Kell and get the hell out of here.* He glanced briefly back at Ava, who was following him quietly. Logan brought up the rear.

Jed turned left at the end of the hallway, halting in front of the last door and inclined his head. *Right here.*

Tristan nodded and moved into position. Logan took up the other side of the door, giving the go-ahead. Tristan opened the door carefully, silently and walked inside, followed by Logan.

"Well, well," said a masculine voice. "We've been waiting for you."

At the end of the room stood a tall, slender man flanked by about two dozen Erosian guards. A young man was tied to a chair, his head bowed, his body marked by bruises and dried blood.

"Kell," Ava gasped in shock. She turned furious eyes at the man in the middle of the guards. "Damn you, Malek."

The man Ava called Malek smiled with malicious glee. "You left me no choice, my beautiful Ava. When you escaped from the isolation cell, I knew you would come for Kell sooner or later." His hard glance slid over Tristan. "I just didn't expect you to bring *friends*."

Ava glared at him with hate in her eyes. "Let him go."

"You know I can't do that," Malek replied, crossing his arms over his chest. "This is all his fault, by the way. He wouldn't tell me where you were."

Tears pricked at the corner of Ava's eyes. "That's because he didn't know."

Malek's gaze hardened. "I'm going to be magnanimous, Ava. I'm going to let your friends go free. But you, you stay with me." The way he said it left no doubt what he was going to do to her.

Tristan shook his head. "I don't think so. How about you let Kell go and we won't kill any of you?"

An ugly laugh erupted from Malek. "You're in no position to bargain, whoever you are. You're surrounded.

Even if you manage to get outside, they'll shoot you on sight." He raised his eyebrow, looking at Ava with ill-concealed lust. "I've changed my mind, Ava. Obviously, you wouldn't be suitable for the Neehaleese king. I think I'll keep you as my bed-mate."

Her lips curled with disgust. "Never."

Jed and I will take care of the guards, Logan offered. *Tris, no doubt you'll take care of Malek?*

Absolutely, Tristan replied with barely leashed anger. He could gleefully wring the man's neck for the way he was looking at Ava. Pulling her behind him, he faced Malek. "We're taking Kell and Ava with us. I don't want this to get ugly. If I were you, I wouldn't stop us."

Malek gave him a disdainful stare. "You're sure that you'll get out of here alive?"

Tristan gave his men an imperceptible signal. With a ruthless skill honed by years of fighting, they attacked the guards. It happened fast, with not a single shot fired. A cacophony of groans and grunts filled the room, and for a while, chaos reigned. The Erosian guards didn't know what hit them. Karn'alian Cyborgs were highly trained in combat, whether with their bare hands or with weapons. Their strength was vastly superior to humanoids. In the end, the guards all lay on the floor, lolling weakly, or were rendered unconscious.

Malek stared, horrified at the speed with which they'd disposed of his men. He brought out a radio and called for more guards. But before he could finish speaking, Tristan threw a small, curved knife. The pierced radio fell, useless, to the floor, crackling loudly.

A flicker of fear crossed Malek's face as Tristan began to advance toward him. He took a hasty step back. "You'll never get out of here alive."

Tristan grabbed him by the neck and pushed him against the wall. He stuck his face close to the terrified Erosian and said in a low, menacing voice, "I'm tempted to snap your neck in two for the way you're looking at *my* woman."

Malek gurgled noisily, his face turning red.

"I'm taking her and her brother away from this planet. And if I even *think* you're following us, I'll come back here and finish you off. Do we understand each other?" he asked.

Nodding, Malek choked and gasped. Tristan simply let go, letting him slide to the floor, limp and shaking. He dismissed Malek and turned to find Logan and Jed untying the slowly rousing Kell.

Ava rushed to his side. "Kell, are you all right?"

Kell slowly opened his eyes and blinked, eyes widening despite the cuts around his eyes. "Ava?" he rasped. He glanced around in bewilderment, his gaze landing on the three Cyborgs. "What happened? Who are you?"

Upon seeing Kell's face, Tristan stiffened. Logan and Jed looked shocked. Logan was the first one to recover. "Tristan?"

"I know," Tristan replied grimly. "I see it, too. But we don't have time right now. Let's get out of here."

Feeling the undercurrents between the three men, Ava glanced at Tristan questioningly. "What is it?"

His lips thinned. "Later. Logan, take Kell." He waited a moment as Logan helped Kell to his feet. He frowned as once again his eyes fell on Ava's brother. Could it be that they really didn't know who they were? This was big. Bigger than simple retrieval of surviving Karn'alians. For Kell was the very image of the Prime Ruler.

Ava and Kell were the long-lost children of the Prime Ruler of Karn'al.

* * * * *

Tristan stared with tight-faced grimness at the vast openness of space outside the operations room of the Destroyer.

"Is it possible that it's them?" Jed asked. "It was believed they were killed while trying to escape the Pagans."

"Apparently not," Logan stated dryly. "I don't think there's any mistaking Kell. He's the very image of his father."

"I know," Tristan agreed quietly. "The Prime Ruler hadn't yet ascended to power at the time the Pagans invaded. According to the elders, he sent his wife and twin babies on the last ship to escape Karn'al, the ship that was never heard from again."

Jed whistled. "He'll be very surprised and pleased when we get back with them."

Logan nodded. "No doubt. But his wife died some time back, right, Tris?"

Tristan nodded. "I'll have to talk to Ava. This won't be easy to accept."

"What won't be easy to accept?" Ava asked as she walked in, catching the last of Tristan's statement. When no one answered, she continued. "Something's going on. I'd like to know what it is."

"Jed and I have to prepare for our landing," Logan hastily spoke up. "We'll leave you to it, Tris."

Tristan waited until the two men were safely out of the room before facing Ava with a sigh. "I was hoping to wait until we got to Karn'al before I talked to you."

She gave him a wary look. "What is it?"

He ran his hands through his hair, wanting to make this easy for her. "Did you know your father?"

Ava visibly stiffened. "He died a long time ago, that's all I know."

"He's not dead." He didn't know how to break the truth to her that would lessen the shock. There was no other way but to come right out and say it. "Your father is the Prime Ruler of Karn'al."

Tristan began to worry when she didn't speak, didn't even move. When she did, her voice was cold. "You're mistaken. My father is dead."

He sighed. "I'm not mistaken. Kell looks remarkably like him, Ava. So much so, that when we saw your brother, we knew instantly who your father is." Tristan took her hand in his, rubbing her soft palm. "He thought you were dead."

She tossed her head. "Is that why he never bothered to look for us?" she asked, bitterness lacing her tone. "My mother cried every day, Tristan. She didn't think I knew, but she could never quite hide the loneliness she felt. He didn't care to find out what happened to his family. He didn't bother to look for us." She turned away, hugging herself tightly.

Tristan shifted to stand behind her, wrapping his arms around her. He didn't know how else to comfort her. "I wouldn't presume to know all the answers, Ava. All I know is, he believed you were dead. If it makes you feel better, he's never mated with another woman, nor has he sired any other children." He kissed the soft shell of her ear. "Your father is a good man. Give him a chance to explain when you meet him."

She leaned against him. "I'm not sure I *want* to meet him."

"You can't avoid that. People will take one look at Kell and realize who he is."

The sigh that blew from her lips was full of sadness. "Can't you take me somewhere else? I don't think I can do this."

"My duty is to take you back home." His answer was matter-of-fact. He wanted her to see there was no other way. "Even more so now that I know your real identity. I have to take you back to Karn'al."

She sniffled, a sound which tore at his heart. "I have to let Kell know."

Admiration blossomed inside him. He didn't doubt she was brave enough to face whatever came. "Don't worry. I'll be right there with you if you need me," he assured her softly. Something tugged at his heart, something he never expected to feel. If he could take her hurt away, he would. He never wanted anything to hurt her again. Tristan refused to examine exactly why he felt that way. Like so much in his life, he accepted it with grace and without question. If Ava was the woman destined to be his mate, then so be it. He would claim her as his as soon as they arrived on Karn'al.

Chapter Seven

Killian was his name, and he was the Prime Ruler of Karn'al. Ava faced her father after so many years. She swallowed and lifted her chin. *I can do this. I'm not scared.* He was tall and silver-haired, his body still strong and muscular beneath the flowing robes. Her heart ached as she looked at Kell standing next to her. Father and son looked so much alike, there was no mistaking Kell as the progeny of the Prime Ruler.

She held herself stiff as he hugged her. "My daughter, I have despaired of ever seeing you again." Were those tears that glistened in his eyes?

Killian drew a deep breath. "Your mother? She passed peacefully?"

Ava nodded with a jerk of her head. "She died in her sleep."

For a moment, stark sadness shone in his weathered, still-handsome face. "Aleesia was my first and only love. No other woman would do for me." He gave a small nod, composing himself once more. "I told her to take you somewhere safe, and that I would come for all of you."

Ava's heart tightened. "But you never came."

"No," he agreed sadly. "I was lost for some time, presumed a casualty of war. I was badly injured and hid out deep in the mountains. By the time I healed and came back, I was informed your mother had taken you on the last ship to escape. A ship that I was told was lost, no survivors reported."

She didn't want to, but Ava felt herself softening toward this man whose pain was so apparent. He couldn't hide the grief he felt upon hearing of her mother's death. Ava found herself wanting to ease some of his pain. "Mother never loved another, if that brings you any comfort. She was devoted to your memory. Although Kell and I never had the chance to know you, we knew she loved you."

Killian swallowed, gripping her hand tightly. "Thank you, my child. My heart aches just looking at you, for you are so like your mother."

Something in her eased, allowing her to breathe lighter. Her eyes fell on her brother, so tall and handsome, looking strong and confident next to Killian. *Oh Mother, how I would give anything for you to be here right now.*

"It will not be easy," she began, hope blooming in her chest. "But I want to get to know you, F-father."

Killian didn't bother to hide the tears in his eyes. "My heart thanks you, Ava. For some reason, the Gods have chosen to bestow upon me a second chance to be with you and Kell. I have no wish to squander it."

He wrapped his arms around her. Ava leaned against him, closing her eyes, feeling his love for her. All the anger and bitterness she had harbored while growing up seemed to melt away with that touch. She realized she wanted to get to know the father that had been denied her by cruel circumstance. This was what her mother would have wanted.

"Everything will be well from here on out," Killian declared gruffly. "Now that I have you and Kell with me, all is well."

* * * * *

Ava was shown to a small dwelling on the outskirts of the city. It was pretty much like the rest of the Karn'alian dwellings — small, square structures identifiable only by a number. It was furnished sparsely, the only furniture being a large bed in the middle of the room. Her escort left her silently, the door closing behind her.

"I was beginning to think you weren't coming."

Ava jumped, whirling around to find Tristan leaning against an open doorway on the far side of the room. "*Tristan.*"

He searched her face intently. "Everything went well?"

She nodded. "Yes. I've decided he's not such a bad man. We were all victims of the chaos that war brings." She blinked in confusion. "Why am I staying here instead of with my father?"

Tristan strolled toward her, looking attractive in a tunic and loose trousers. Out of uniform, he was as devastating as ever. She looked up at him when he stopped a few feet from her.

"This is where I live," he informed her, looking deep into her eyes. "You were brought here because I've claimed you, Ava. In the eyes of all of Karn'al, you're my mate."

She cocked her head. "Don't I have a say in this?"

A shadow crossed his face, too fast for her to discern what it meant. "You can deny my claim. If you wish to do that, all you have to do is return to your father and declare it so." He caressed her cheek with his hand. "By doing so, you're declaring yourself free for another man to claim you, to lay his hands on you." He lowered his head, brushing his lips against hers. "To fuck you."

Her breath hitched. "What does it mean when you claim me?"

He licked the corners of her lips. "If you agree, we will be mated in a traditional Karn'alian ceremony." He kissed her deeply. By the time he withdrew, her breath was coming in quick gasps.

She felt bereft when he moved away. "If you agree, there are some things you need to know about mating." He took a moment before he spoke. "Cyborgs are more than just comrades, we're blood brothers. When one of us mates with a woman, we have to fulfill what is called the Ritual of Acceptance."

She frowned, not understanding. "Ritual of Acceptance?"

He held her gaze directly. "You have to join with me and one other in the ritual."

Shock coursed through her system. "By joining, you mean—?"

"Yes. For one time only, I and a comrade of my choosing, one who is closest to me, will join us in our bed to mate with you as well."

Her knees weakened. Erotic images assailed her at his words. She remembered when Logan and Jed watched her make love with Tristan. She could feel the same thrill of excitement snaking through her system. She really shouldn't be so excited at the thought.

But the possibility *did* excite her. The thought of another, maybe Logan or Jed, pleasuring her along with Tristan was very tempting.

She swallowed, trying to hide what she was feeling. Would he think her wanton for wanting to do that? "That's all right with you?" she managed to ask through dry lips.

"It's the Karn'alian way. More so with the Cyborgs, Ava. If I die in combat, one of my comrades will step in and take care of you, provide for you, protect you." He looked so calm, so collected, that it was hard for her to see what he was thinking. "It is required that we do it once. Only once." For a brief moment, he allowed his true feelings to show. "Because I don't think I could bear it if I had to share you every night."

She took a step toward him.

He warded her off with a shake of his head. "I need your answer."

Did she really have any other choice? Tristan gave her incredible pleasure. He was gentle, he was considerate. The heat they generated was unbelievable. Could she really allow another man to take his place? The thought was repulsive to her. She didn't want any other man. She wanted him and him alone.

"More than anything else in this world," she began softly, walking toward him, "I want to be your mate." Her hands crept around his neck. "Only you, Tristan. Nobody else." She touched her lips to his. "You make me feel things I've never felt before."

Something close to relief flickered in his face. "Then it's done. You're mine, Ava."

Ava buried her face in his chest. "Same goes for you. You're all mine." She burrowed closer to the warmth of his body. "This ritual, when does it happen?"

"Right now."

Moisture pooled in her lower belly, rendering her limbs useless. She leaned into him, already aroused at the thought. "Have you decided who?"

He groaned and tunneled his fingers through her hair. "I don't know what I ever did to deserve you. But I swear on my life, that I will do everything in my power to make you happy, Ava."

Sheer joy blossomed in her heart. "You already make me happy, Tristan."

Cupping her buttocks, he pulled her up against his already stiff cock. He led her to the bed, stripping her of her clothes. When she was naked, he bent and tongued her nipple. Her breath hitched in her throat. She pulled him closer, loving the push and pull of his mouth, getting unbearably aroused. But all too soon, he stepped back. Shaking, she tried to remain still as he opened a drawer. The desire coursing through her blended thick and fast in her bloodstream. She had no resistance to the feeling. She was already wet. There was no hiding that fact from him.

He had a black silk cloth in his hand when he turned back to her. "Turn around."

A rush of excitement swelled inside her. She bit her lip as he wrapped the cloth around her eyes and blindfolded her.

"Tristan?"

"Trust me." His voice was low and gentle. "This is all for you, Ava. I want to make this as special as I can."

She shivered as he knotted the cloth securely. Cool air whispered over her skin, tightening her nipples and sparking an almost unbearable ache in her pussy. The door swished open. Her head came up.

"Who's here?" she asked in a whisper, her voice trembling with anticipation.

Cool lips touched her nape. "It's all right. Just relax."

She melted against Tristan, loving his familiar touch. The rough pads of his fingers slid down her side, coming to a stop on her hips. She jumped as a new set of hands drifted over her breasts, lightly brushing her nipples. She moaned. "Tristan?"

His low, sensuous voice rasped from somewhere beside her. "I'm right here."

A pair of hands settled lightly on the curve of her waist. She instinctively knew it wasn't Tristan. It felt different. They drifted down to her mound, catching some of her moisture in a quick swipe.

She whimpered. Flames licked wherever they touched her body. It was tortuous to stand there and absorb the sensations brought about by so many fingers. Her feelings were heightened by being blindfolded and not seeing who was touching her. She didn't know what to expect or what was coming. She succumbed to the feeling of total helplessness that was assailing her. Total surrender, that's what she was giving them. She was surrendering to the pleasure the two of them would give her.

Somebody—perhaps Tristan?—guided her to lie down on the bed. Heart hammering, she lay quiescent and expectant, waiting for what was surely to come. When it came, it was where she hardly expected it to originate. A firm set of lips kissed her feet, laving her toes with soft licks.

Ava inhaled sharply. She never knew how erotic it was to have her toes sucked. She moaned and shifted on the bed.

"Don't move." Tristan's harsh order came over her head. She looked up, tilting her face toward the sound, seeking him. He laughed softly, taking her wrists in each of his hands, pulling them over her head, wrapping her fingers around the thick headboard. "Hold on to that."

Lips skimmed her middle, laving her navel with languorous licks. Her nipples tightened in the cool air, already expecting their fair share of attention. But the lips headed below, right toward her sopping pussy. Ava rubbed her legs against the cool sheets restlessly, opening them wide. A very pleased, very male laugh reached her ears before a damp tongue swooped between her slick folds and sought her clit.

Ava reared off the bed, the touch electrifying her. She moaned, not in the least satisfied. The moan turned into a gasp when her nipples were pulled, teeth gently raking over the sensitive tips. Her pussy was not spared, the stiff clit laved over and over again by a delightfully rough tongue.

"Amazing," a masculine voice exclaimed. "Her pussy is indeed hot."

She flushed, vaguely recognizing the voice. But her senses whirled dizzily, bombarded on two fronts. She almost let go of the headboard, momentarily forgetting Tristan's instruction to hold on. After one particularly tender bite on her clit, she gasped, only to feel a very thick, very erect cock nudge her lips. Her senses whirled—she didn't know who'd taken possession of her pussy or whose cock was at her lips. She no longer cared.

With a soft moan, she opened her lips. The cock was huge, the tip broad and warm as she enveloped it in her mouth. Spurred on by the grunt of pleasure at her action, she applied herself to pleasuring the cock. With her tongue, she licked it up and down, pausing to savor the thick vein that pulsed from the base of the shaft. A big hand pillowed her head, raising her slightly for a better angle. He fed her the cock as deep as she could take it. Again and again, the cock swelled even more inside her mouth.

Ava was no longer aware of her surroundings. All she could focus on was the pleasure they were giving her, assaulting her senses without mercy. A pair of callused hands pushed her legs wide apart, a warm male body settling in between. His tongue was a weapon for which she had no resistance. He was a master at licking and exploring her tender, giving pussy.

She'd never had so much attention given to her breasts. They were pulled and tugged in an erotic massage. The tips were highly sensitive to the slightest touch. They were heavy and tingling from being kneaded and caressed, shaped and squeezed.

So much was happening at once, she couldn't take it anymore. With a small scream, she tore her lips from the cock as she came. On and on it went, until the violent tremors subsided and she was left gasping for air. Limp and weak, she slumped back on the bed.

The mattress dipped as the men shifted. Somebody picked her up and positioned her on top of a warm body. She trembled, still reeling from the aftershock. A tortured moan was wrung from her as a thick cock pushed its way inside her pussy, slipping all the way to her womb in one stroke. Her mind spun. Was it possible to die from too much pleasure? A soft whimper of protest hovered on her lips. The huge cock inside her was barely moving.

A harsh breath was expelled loudly beneath her. "It's...too hot," a male voice gasped. It was moments later before he moved inside her. With deliberate movements, the cock went in and out, deeper and deeper, each time a little harder. "I've never had a pussy this hot."

In the next moment, Ava lost her breath as she felt something cold and slippery applied to her rear. She froze as one, then two fingers worked the thick substance around and inside, their entrance made easy by the lubrication. Before long, she'd accepted their entire length, stretched and slick. But too quickly, they were gone. She gasped as she felt the broad tip of a cock working its way inside the tight ring of muscle. "Ohhhh."

The blindfold covering her eyes was pulled off. Trapped between two male bodies, Ava looked down to see Logan under her. His face was twisted with pleasure, his hands anchoring her hips. She looked over her shoulder and met Tristan's hot gaze. The head of his cock finally slipped in and she cried out at the intense pleasure that followed the momentary pain. "Tristan!"

Inch by tormenting inch, he worked his cock inside her ass until he was all the way in. She sucked in her breath with a sharp hiss, feeling utterly possessed. "Tristan," she whimpered.

"By the Gods, Ava, it feels so good," he rasped, wrapping his arms around her and seeking the jiggling mounds of her breasts.

In unison, Tristan and Logan began to move. Thrusting in and out, adopting a rhythm that drove her insane. Throwing her head back, she panted. She was no longer her own person, but an instrument of pleasure for the two men. It was exhilarating to be the center of such torrid attention, every thrust a push toward the edge, toward the approaching precipice.

With a gentle touch, Tristan drew her hair over her shoulder and kissed her shoulder. A stark contrast to his escalating strokes. She heard animal-like noises echoing in the room and realized it was her.

"Tris, I'm not going to last long," Logan grunted, tunneling his cock deep in her pussy.

In response, Tristan tugged her hair and angled her face for his kiss. He fucked her with little gentleness, his hips slamming against her buttocks with mind-numbing intensity, again and again.

Her orgasm, when it came, hit her with such force that she tore her lips from his and screamed. "Tristan!" Huge waves of pleasure slammed into her as she shuddered violently. She was only dimly aware of Logan pumping his seed into her. But it was Tristan she was aware of. She knew the exact moment he stiffened behind her and uttered a soft curse as his cock clenched inside her ass. Tears came to her eyes at the immense combination of pleasure and pain that streaked through her body, centering on where her body was joined with Tristan's. Exhausted, she slumped back against him as he shifted, lifting her off Logan. The slide of the other man's cock out of her pussy made her shiver with remembered pleasure. She moaned as Tristan slipped out of her ass and he laid them down on the bed.

After a long moment, Logan stood up and dressed. "My gratitude, Tristan," he murmured. "I can't remember the last time I've had so much pleasure." His warm gaze fell on Ava. "He tried to warn me that your pussy was— unusual. I regret I will only have the privilege to feel it this once." He ran his hand down her cheek before he left as silently as he came in.

Tristan leaned over her. "Are you all right?" he asked with gentle concern when they were finally alone.

Although she was sure her cheeks were red, it really was too late to feel embarrassed. The pleasure she had derived from the experience was proof that she had enjoyed it. "I'm wonderful."

He chuckled. "I'm glad you enjoyed it." He pushed a damp tendril behind her ear. "Although I must warn you, I will not do that again." His arms tightened around her. "You're mine, Ava. I couldn't bear it if I had to share you all the time."

The possessiveness in his tone didn't bother her, instead she reveled in it. "It was fun tonight." She kissed the corner of his lips. "But I don't think I'd want to do it on a regular basis either." She frowned. "This ritual thing, I don't have to reciprocate by sharing you with another woman, do I?" Her tone clearly indicated she wouldn't find any pleasure in that.

A pleased grin parted his lips. "No, you don't have to share me." He drew back and looked at her with concern. "Are you sure about this, Ava? My life is not an easy one. I will be sent out on missions frequently, to faraway places. I don't want you to regret being my mate." His eyes clouded. "I wouldn't like it, but I would understand if you would rather stay with your father and get to know him."

Ava couldn't believe this big, strong Cyborg of hers was showing a rare moment of insecurity. "My father and I have a lifetime to get to know each other. I want to stay with you, Tristan. I wouldn't want it any other way." She kissed him. A feeling of love welled up in her chest, threatening to bubble over. Her eyes memorized his strong, handsome features and her heart melted. "I'm so glad you found me."

His face was somber. "You were meant for me. How else can you explain that I found you on a world millions of miles away from Karn'al?"

The light of love shone brightly in his eyes, there for her — for anybody — to see.

Her life had taken a turn for the better. Pleasure Planet seemed a thousand miles away, her lonely existence just a memory. Kell was now the heir to a kingdom. Her brother had shown remarkable courage and strength facing the changes in their life. His relationship with Killian was guarded and wary, but Ava was positive that would change soon. Already she could see a tentative bond forming between them all.

As for her, she found love with her very own Cyborg, a warrior sworn to protect and love her all the rest of their days.

About the author

Beverly Havlir writes her books surrounded by plush pink and white heart-shaped pillows and soft, sexy music playing in the background. She plots her stories dressed in sheer, silky lingerie while eating bonbons and sipping champagne.

Now for a dash of reality…

After running around doing totally unglamorous chores all day, Beverly writes at night when all is quiet and she is (at last!) alone. Exhaustion disappears as soon as she sits down in front of her computer, doing what she loves best: writing stories that bring women's fantasies to life.

Beverly welcomes mail from readers. You can write to her c/o Ellora's Cave Publishing at 1056 Home Ave. Akron, Oh. 44310-3502.

Also by Beverly Havlir

The Abduction of Emma
Bodyguard
Taming Alex

Why an electronic book?

We live in the Information Age—an exciting time in the history of human civilization in which technology rules supreme and continues to progress in leaps and bounds every minute of every hour of every day. For a multitude of reasons, more and more avid literary fans are opting to purchase e-books instead of paperbacks. The question to those not yet initiated to the world of electronic reading is simply: *why?*

1. *Price.* An electronic title at Ellora's Cave Publishing and Cerridwen Press runs anywhere from 40-75% less than the cover price of the <u>exact same title</u> in paperback format. Why? Cold mathematics. It is less expensive to publish an e-book than it is to publish a paperback, so the savings are passed along to the consumer.

2. *Space.* Running out of room to house your paperback books? That is one worry you will never have with electronic novels. For a low one-time cost, you can purchase a handheld computer designed specifically for e-reading purposes. Many e-readers are larger than the average handheld, giving you plenty of screen room. Better yet, hundreds of titles can be stored within your new library—a single microchip. (Please note that Ellora's Cave and Cerridwen Press does not endorse any specific brands. You can check our website at www.ellorascave.com or

www.cerridwenpress.com for customer recommendations we make available to new consumers.)

3. *Mobility*. Because your new library now consists of only a microchip, your entire cache of books can be taken with you wherever you go.

4. *Personal preferences are accounted for*. Are the words you are currently reading too small? Too large? Too...**ANNOYING**? Paperback books cannot be modified according to personal preferences, but e-books can.

5. *Instant gratification*. Is it the middle of the night and all the bookstores are closed? Are you tired of waiting days—sometimes weeks—for online and offline bookstores to ship the novels you bought? Ellora's Cave Publishing sells instantaneous downloads 24 hours a day, 7 days a week, 365 days a year. Our e-book delivery system is 100% automated, meaning your order is filled as soon as you pay for it.

Those are a few of the top reasons why electronic novels are displacing paperbacks for many an avid reader. As always, Ellora's Cave and Cerridwen Press welcomes your questions and comments. We invite you to email us at service@ellorascave.com, service@cerridwenpress.com or write to us directly at: 1056 Home Ave. Akron OH 44310-3502.

Discover for yourself why readers can't get enough of the multiple award-winning publisher Ellora's Cave. Whether you prefer e-books or paperbacks, be sure to visit EC on the web at www.ellorascave.com for an erotic reading experience that will leave you breathless.

www.ellorascave.com

Printed in the United States
96062LV00001B/199/A